Naked Soul

A NOVELLA

Symire Jones

Copyright © 2018 by Symire Jones

Cover design by Steve Azzara

Photograph and Illustrations copyright © by Zhon Yancy

ISBN: 978-0-9600-6210-2

Thank you

To my SUN Machai Grant, thank you so much for being my inspiration throughout my writing process. *Naked Soul* would not have been completed if I didn't have the honor of being your mother. You have pushed me beyond my limit and brought nothing but peace, joy, lots of laughter and smiles to my life. You have been so patient with me during the endless days and nights I was glued to my laptop writing. Mommy promises to always love you and protect you. I'll be your mommy first and your best friend second. This world is so big and at times you may feel lost or lonely, but I will always be here for you. Even if I am not here physically, I live in your heart and I will carry you in my heart forever. In this lifetime, you will experience trial and error, but remain optimistic and always find the good in the bad. I PRAY God blesses you with a life full of health and happiness. You have given me life, and there is no greater super power God could have blessed me with than the super power of creating you.

Dedication

To all of the strong women who have been broken. There is a man waiting to gather those pieces and love the shit out of you. May we never give up on love, may we never settle, and may we all get our happily ever after because it does exist.

Prologue

by Patricia Wilder

Behind every storm there's a quiet rain. Behind every secret there's a reason. Behind every lie there's a mystery. Behind every love there's hate. Behind every truth there's a lie. But when will the reason unfold? When will the mystery be solved?

When will lies turn into understanding? How can we break something down to the point where there's nothing to hide, no one to fear, and no pain to bare? When will we understand why we feel pain? Or why someone close always hurts us the most? What is the logic of life? What exactly is the point? What is the fulfillment of going through the struggle and dying? Where does life lead you? Some people may say it all depends on how you live your life. But does it really?

First you're born and then you die. Maybe some lives go faster than others. Only because their fulfillment of life was done or because their logic of life wasn't logical or even because someone else's logic was embedded into them.

When are we going to see that the best way to live our lives is our way. When are we going to realize happiness is the only thing we struggle for? Is it hard to see that the only battle that exists is within ourselves? Is this the real logic of life? How can we say for sure? We can't, so all I can say is life boils down to logic, and if you aren't logical about what you want, then you have no fulfillment of life.

Chapter 1

May 2013-Vanessa

Five forty-five in the morning. I woke up naked and frantic. The arms that held me didn't feel like my husband's, didn't smell like my husband's, and definitely were not the same complexion as my husband's.

The buzz from last night's cognac still lingered in my head and the sweet sound of the birds singing to announce the arrival of the sun did nothing to soothe my headache. The walls closed in on me; it felt as though the mirrored ceiling seemed ready to shatter and fall.

I closed my eyes, and struggled to catch my breath, praying this wasn't happening. The sweet mixture of fresh, earthy aromas filled the room. They were beautiful, but they were foreign, unsettling. The fragile smell of last night's downpour entwined with the scents of spring, and masculine cologne.

Sitting up and leaning back against the headboard, I stared at the man lying beside me. Sliding my hand under the covers allowed me to feel his bare skin; I detected he was just as naked as I was. Lifting the covers a bit higher, I peeked underneath.

Another attractive feature of his caught my attention. *"Mmmm,"* I uttered while biting down on my bottom lip. Lying strong against his hard body was his elongated, fairly thick chocolate penis. It was obvious the sun wasn't the only thing that had risen that morning.

His legs reached to the edge of the bed. Three more inches and they would have dangled off the edge. The word inches danced freely in my head. So tempting. I wanted to consume all of his inches inside of me again, even though I was still sore from the night before. Even though I shouldn't have been in this bed at all.

I eased myself back under the sheet, trying not to jostle him in the process. Watching us together in the mirror above brought a rush of memories that was pleasurable and sickening at the same time. Glancing at my own reflection, my own beauty had turned into a "beast." My once silky-straight hair was now untidy and tangled. Patting it down, I made an effort to improve my appearance before he woke up, but it was a lost cause. *So much for my wash and set.* I laid there with matted, gnarled, after-sex hair. Such a mess I couldn't even run my fingers through. *The better the sex, the messier the hair,* I thought. *Next time I'll skip the professional blowout if I'm going to get my back blown out.*

I felt incredibly ashamed at the idea of another man having me. Guilt washed over me, but there was an onslaught of other mixed emotions at my guilty pleasure of a man enjoying the depths of me. It felt all too good to have someone value my flaws and my imperfections making me feel wanted again. Most of my thoughts were a blur cluttering my mind. *I'm really in another man's bed.* I remembered watching my facial expressions while he fucked me hard. Just that memory alone made me shiver with excitement.

Somehow, the sins I'd committed didn't stop me from lusting after this man. The sunlight eased its way through the curtains and kissed his Hennessey skin. I could not stop admiring him, feeling the desire to kiss him too. I tried to imagine the taste of him now that I was sober. His body looked like cognac itself. The flavor of his rich melanin skin with red undertones would hide all of his flaws—if he had any.

The sun's rays created a flash when they hit the diamond on my ring finger, reminding me of the vows I'd taken to be loyal and faithful, for better or for worse. I gently placed my hands over my face, rubbing my eyes to wake myself from what I hoped might be a dream.

I pulled the covers over my head, trying to hide from my shame. A moment later, the fine man beside me laughed quietly. I peeked out and saw his grin—pearly white teeth that contrasted with his complexion. He yawned while stretching his arms widely. As he rolled over, his hand gripped my waist and pulled me toward him. Suddenly uncomfortable at his touch, I squirmed away and he released me.

"Good morning, beautiful."

"Morning Lance," I mumbled, filled with a sense of regret when the stench of my morning breath invaded the space between us. "What did we do?" I asked, as if I didn't already know.

Lance gently massaged my upper thigh. "*We* did what *you* asked." I looked at him, confused. "You asked me to make you forget," he said in a low voice.

"Forget? Forget what?" I asked irritably.

He reached for my left hand and played with the pear-shaped ring on my finger. "Did you enjoy your night?"

"Excuse me?" I snatched my hand back from him in disbelief that he could be so insensitive. And yet, I realized how turned on I was in that moment. *Pathetic.* "I'm happily married and I need to go so let's not pretend--"

"Let's not pretend you didn't want me as much as I wanted you," he said, cutting me off. "Happily married or not."

"I agreed to meet you for dinner and drinks only," I snapped back at him. "This was not supposed to go any further and you know it." *How did a friendly dinner turn into a night of fucking anyways?* A large and heavy white Persian cat leaped on me, interrupting my thoughts and calming my anxiety. Sniffing my scent, she carefully walked around me, purring as her body rippled with style and grace. Rolling on her back, she exposed her stomach, inviting me to gently rub it.

Every emotion I felt was written on my face, and probably seeing my guilt, Lance tried to lighten the mood. "But it did happen and you can't take your pussycat back," he said, while joining in on the belly rub. He turned his attention to the cat. "Right Snowball?" he asked, followed by a burst of laughter.

I didn't find anything funny about any of this. "I'm glad I could make you laugh, Lance. You and Snowball."

"Please, Vanessa. Let's not play victim here. You were very much in control last night."

I stared at him with a blank expression. He was right about that. "Okay, well it was a mistake. Just as long as you know this was a mistake." I kept my tone cold, trying to make him feel just as worthless as I felt. But the truth was, it was a beautiful mistake.

He sat on the edge of the bed. I could feel his energy completely shift as he turned his back on me and sucked his teeth. "I hope you don't go around making a lot of these mistakes," he said. The scratches on his back reminded me of my perfectly manicured nails, raking into his deep, dark skin as I begged him to allow me to feel all of him.

As I scanned the room in search for my panties and bra, I spotted wine glasses tipped over at the side of the bed. Lance quickly stood up and pulled on his boxer briefs. He turned on the music that had been playing during last night's rendezvous—before climbing back into bed. "Life's too short for regrets. Happiness is too important to be brushed off, and it's too early in the morning to be arguing with you. So go back to sleep and wake up on the right side of the bed."

"How can I wake up on the right side of the bed when I woke up in the wrong bed to begin with?" I gave him a quick smack to the back of the head then threw my body down on his bed. Feeling such embarrassment and disgust, I buried my head under the white plush pillow. The comfort from the cold pillow was snatched away within seconds when his body vigorously pressed against mine.

I couldn't resist. I dove into his dark brown eyes as he gently pushed my hair behind my ears. It was something about the way Lance looked at me. It was something about the way his eyes slow-danced up and down my body. I enjoyed his style and the way he articulated himself in such a masculine fashion. It seemed he was fascinated by the very same imperfections my husband seemed so disgusted by.

"Do you know your worth? Because once you understand it, no one in this world can ever make you feel worthless. Not me, not your husband. Nobody. Even if last night was a mistake for you and you ended up in the wrong bed, you made me feel like I did more than just exist, so thank you."

In the silence that followed, I became intensely aware

of my heart beating. I had fallen in love with this man and it was at that moment that I forgot about the rules of the game. "I love you," I said, the words flowing effortlessly from my tongue. My stomach twisted in knots, like it did when I rode a rollercoaster, a ride I rarely ever enjoyed.

Why did you do that? Why, why, why? I was in such an awkward space now. *Say something, Vanessa. Say something now!* The words screamed out loud in my head. I glanced at Snowball; she seemed to be waiting for his answer just as I was.

Finally, Lance spoke. "I want you to fall back in love with yourself first before you fall in love with me, or anyone else for that matter."

For a second I lay there, conflicted between wanting an encore of last night and giving him a piece of my mind for not telling me he loved me back. Even Snowball seemed disappointed at his answer. She hissed and sprang off the bed, giving him a piece of her mind for me, and melted into the shadows. I struggled to say something but my words felt like a stone in my throat. Clearly, it was time to go.

Without any more hesitation, I snatched his white sheet and twirled around in it for warmth as the spring breeze blew through the open window. I couldn't help but glance back at him, taking a second to admire his fully exposed body. I found myself in awe. Just the sight of him sent chills up my spine—or maybe it was because the window was open.

I quickly ran into the bathroom to get dressed. Two used condoms floated in the toilet. All I could think about was my husband. *What kind of wife am I?*

Once I pulled myself together, I grabbed my keys and raced to the front of the unfamiliar home. I was gasping for breath by the time I got to my car. I started up the engine and blasted music, side-swiping Lance's black BMW as I passed it. As if things couldn't get any more complicated.

When I had gotten some distance away, I had to pull over. Sitting in my car half-dressed, feeling disoriented and disgusted, I had to wonder how I had allowed this to happen. I was only one year into my marriage, but maybe this tryst has been a long time coming—and God knows I anticipated it.

For the past few months I've lived in misery trying to please a man who seemed to no longer love me. Now, the one time I decided to find my own pleasure, I find myself pulled over at the side of the road wracked with regret and guilt.

I told myself what my best friend Zoe would have said in this situation: "Girl, pull yourself together. You decided to do something that made you feel good. You deserve that and don't you dare shed another tear. Whatever happened never happened." Her words soothed my mind and my soul.

Facing the reality that I had just betrayed the vows that I once held so sacred seemed unbearable. Lance was not the man I chose to marry, neither is he the man I would now have to go home and answer to. *What kind of wife am I?* I repeatedly asked myself until it began to sound like a chant.

What I had done could potentially break up my happy home. "*Happy* home?" I asked myself, feeling confused. Saying those words out loud made me realize I didn't have a fucking happy home and that this was all Chase's fault.

CHAPTER 2

Vanessa, December 2012

Five Months Earlier

Our mornings had turned cold, and, like our marriage, the morning was frigid. It was past six thirty, and my lips had yet to receive a birthday kiss from my husband. I woke to find his side of the bed made up, as if he'd never come home. I shared a bed with a man whose love was diminishing by the day. I shared a home with a stranger who I shared only memories with. The optimistic doctor who fixes hearts couldn't fix his own heart to love me again.

I decided to call Chase's cell phone and was startled when I heard a faint rhythmic vibration coming from the living room. At that moment, I realized our marriage was in jeopardy. We were newlyweds sleeping in separate rooms and I couldn't tell you why. This was all new to me, and brought on feelings of regret and confusion.

I didn't understand how we had gotten to this point in our marriage so fast. I was okay with the honeymoon phase fading away -- that kind of thing doesn't last forever. The butterflies in my stomach had died and I wanted badly to bring them back to life, but I couldn't do it on my own.

Chase's love seemed like it was slowly turning into hate, and he couldn't hide it anymore. I, on the other hand, was good at faking smiles when I felt like crying; at pretending to be happy when I felt sad. But I couldn't pretend that I didn't love Chase anymore because I did.

I staggered out of the bed. The hardwood floor was bitterly cold against my bare feet. I slipped them into socks, noticing my nail polish was chipped. *Ugh. I badly need a pedicure.* I'd been so caught up in Chase, I'd begun neglecting myself.

I made my way into the living room to find Chase peacefully sleeping there. I paused, contemplating if I should wake him up to come to bed. My stomach burned with jealousy as I watched the blanket tightly hug him. I couldn't help but kneel down next to him and gently kiss his pouted lips. "What do I have to do for you to love me again?" I quietly asked him as he slept. "For you to want me again? For you to touch me again?"

I then carefully lay on top of him while pulling him into a close and comforting embrace. I stayed there for a moment, curling my arms underneath him. Taking some deep breaths, I relaxed my body into his. I would have given anything for this moment to last forever.

I rested my head onto his heaving chest and listened to my favorite tune play -- the beat of his heart. My bottom lip quivered as tears quickly pooled in my dark brown eyes and I allowed them to escape. The torrent of my tears soaked through his white shirt, causing him to awaken. He ran his fingers through my strawberry conditioned hair and softly asked, "Nessa, what's wrong?" Maybe it was the directness of the question but his words only made me cry harder, like the sleet now beating against the window pane.

So many things are wrong, I thought, but I decided not to ruin the moment. Instead, I lay there in silence, wiping my tears away with shaking hands. I took a slight pause and continued to stare up at my husband. Those dark brown eyes, the most beautiful eyes in the world, smiled at me for the first time in a long time. He wiped my cheeks with his fingertips and I finally admitted to him, "I can feel you slipping away." He looked away and I gently kissed the nape of his neck, sweet with his cologne. "Stay with me. Hold me. Make love to me, baby. Please," I begged him.

"I can't, Nessa," he whispered. "Not right now." I ignored him and proceeded traveling down his body. "Vanessa stop!" he shouted, but I couldn't stop.

My tongue was inches away from his anxious penis. Once upon a time, at this point, he would have forcefully pushed his dick into my mouth and I would have willingly sucked him into euphoria. This time was different.

There isn't any way to describe the cold look he gave me before pushing my body off of him. I hit the floor hard, limp, but was comforted by my rug. His action sent chills through my body, paralyzing everything in me, and confirming what I already knew: there was definitely another woman. Our future, which had once held the promise of eternal love, was now fraught with the increasing anxiety that war was coming.

Some might say that to try to revive something already dead is to suffer in misery and false hope. But for me, I believed that if it was true love the heart could be revived and the sparks would fly with even more intensity. I was losing him, but was I wrong for wanting to fight for my marriage, my husband, my friend?

I reached out for him again and he recoiled. "I said not now." He shoved me away.

"Well then, when? When is it a good time to fuck my husband? Do I have to make an appointment? Can't you squeeze me into your busy schedule?"

He got off the couch, then walked away, ignoring me as he had been for the past couple months. Usually I let it go, but this time was different. This time I was ready to fight. "Chase! I am your *wife*. Please fight for us. Why won't you fight for us?"

His silent treatment and "I don't give a fuck" attitude infuriated me. He had disregarded everything I said, then nonchalantly walked into the kitchen and asked if I was hungry. How charming. After he rejected me, he wanted to feed me.

I walked in after him screaming at the top of my lungs. "You know what, Chase?"

He came back at me this time, now unexpectedly showing emotion. "What, Vanessa? What now?" He roared like a fierce lion. "You want me to love you and I can't love you anymore."

I stood there, numb, unable to think clearly as he continued his rant. Frightening me because he never spoke to me like this.

When he quieted, I asked him, "You *can't* love me anymore? Or you *don't* love me anymore?" There was a difference, and I needed it to be clarified. I stood facing him, waiting for him to answer me, but he refused. Instead he continued pouring fresh orange juice into his glass.

"I think we should get a divorce," he said.

My mind was reeling. "A divorce? We just got married and you're asking me for a divorce? Who is she?"

He didn't deny that there was a *her*. Another woman. "It's not like you would know her," he said. After that, every word he spoke enraged me. I decided that he was going to feel my wrath, just like I had felt his. With all my strength, I pulled back my right hand then forcefully whipped it across his face. His left cheek reddened, and I hope it throbbed with as much pain as my hand had felt.

"I'm sorry I wasn't enough for you. I'm sorry that you

had to look elsewhere," I said, unable to control my anger any longer. "I'm so sorry that you were such a weak man that you couldn't fix our broken relationship first. So weak, that you had to stray away from me and into the arms of another woman. I'm so sorry because after five years of being with you and one year of marriage, you can't love me."

Chase stood there and listened to me like a child being scolded by a parent. Anger was written all over my face. If looks could kill I'd be planning a funeral. Frustrated and parched, I reached out and grabbed his orange juice, and took a large sip.

It's crazy how someone can wake up one day and, out of the clear blue sky, decide they don't want to love you anymore. My husband hadn't touched me, had barely even looked at me for months now, which felt like years. Ever since I'd returned from a month of intense medical coursework in Los Angeles for my newest position.

I was tired of trying to figure things out. I was fed up with constantly being denied the right to enter his thoughts and feelings. Truthfully, my back was against the wall.

Pride and egos had made it too late for "sorry"s and "I love you"s.

CHAPTER 3

Vanessa, December 2012

You never remember the hurtful words you say when you're angry until they get thrown back in your face. It's no secret that your words can turn into venom, poisoning your relationship when you're hurt by the one you love.

I had been fighting Chase day in and day out. I was fighting for our marriage to work, but in doing so, I realized I'd only pushed him further away. Fighting wasn't communication – it had just become noise. Now I was ready to shut up and just listen to my husband. I was in desperate need of some quality time together. In this ordinary life of long working hours, I wanted to give him a fairy tale. Maybe I didn't tell him or show him enough that I appreciated him, but I did.

I decided to cook a nice meal to celebrate my birthday. I quickly changed from my scrubs into attire that hugged every curve of my body. Standing in front of the mirror, I envisioned Chase ripping me out of this champagne-colored, rhinestone-studded dress, and enveloping himself in my curves.

As time passed, I became more and more eager. I sat at the head of the table waiting to breathe in his fragrance as he walked through the door. Don't ever believe the way to a man's heart is through his stomach. I fed Chase's mind, body, and soul for years, and that wasn't enough. I wasn't enough.

The fragile rose petals scattered on my dining room table kept me company as I awaited his arrival. They had been gently peeled from their stems, one at a time, as I played the childish game of "he loves me, he loves me not." I'd nearly wounded myself on the stems as I picked the petals away, landing on "he loves me."

When an hour had passed, I realized this special dinner was just another failed attempt at salvaging our love. It felt like a million thorns were penetrating my heart at once, quickly tainting my love with resentment. As much as Chase wanted to ignore these thorns in our marriage, they just couldn't be overlooked. I was praying to build my marriage back because a part of me knew that with these thorns came a rose that was worth all the pain they caused.

By my third glass of wine, hope had somehow taken precedence. They say the third time's the charm, so, I sipped slowly, while giving him the benefit of the doubt. As the minutes passed, my wine continued to disappear, just like Chase.

When he finally returned, his mouth held nothing but liquor and lies. But I had a sweet surprise for him. Daddy always said, "If they don't like what you're bringing to the table let them eat alone," and Momma always said, "One, two, three, there's plenty of fish in the sea." If Chase didn't want to make love to me, I'd just make love to myself with the big black dildo in my dresser.

I headed to the bedroom. He followed me and stood by the door. I lay there on our bed in my birthday suit. Naked, wet, and hungry -- a woman comfortable in her skin. I was taught from a very young age to take care of my body and give it what it needs. My body was looking to be explored and instead it had been rejected and abandoned by the man who vowed to fuck me through better or through worse.

I felt his eyes glued to me, so I put on a show for him. I lost all my inhibitions as I slammed the dildo in and out of me. The plan was to turn Chase on without touching him. I expected Chase to join me but within seconds, my orgasm exploded through me and my body relaxed into the bed. Immediately after, Chase faded away into darkness. That wasn't a surprise. I was getting use to his disappearing acts, but all I wanted was to be found. I knew that in the eyes of my creator I would always be beautiful but that wasn't enough, because in the eyes of my husband, I was unseen and I felt unattractive.

Just then, Zoe called. I had so many missed calls and text messages from her today shouting out "Happy Birthday, you old bitch!" I decided to pick up the call.

"It's just a regular day, Zoe. Nothing special."

"Well get dressed, you old grouch. We about turn this

regular day into a night you'll never forget."

I had always hated the fact that my birthday was in the winter, but bad weather never stopped Zoe from having a good time. She was a free spirit who loved life and the people in it. "I really just want to stay in tonight. Maybe we can do something tomorrow," I replied. Honestly, I wanted to stay home with Chase. I was hoping he'd have a change of heart and maybe we would celebrate.

"Vanessa, it's your birthday. We never miss celebrating a birthday together." Zoe was right. She had moved to Los Angeles when she was about sixteen years old, but even though she was miles away, she made sure to never miss a birthday. Hollywood was exactly where she belonged, a star waiting to blow up. Zoe was always excited to visit New York during the winter season. There was always a lot going on and so much to do. "Get your ass up. I'll be there in twenty minutes and you better not keep me waiting." Zoe was very persistent and always got what she wanted, so I started getting ready.

I blasted *Best Thing I Never Had*, the newest anthem for every girl, but it was more than just an anthem for me. It was empowerment and encouragement to get me through my broken marriage. The music was so loud, I couldn't hear myself think. Chase came into the room. "I'm going to the hospital," he shouted at me over the music. "I'll call you later."

"You better call Becky with the good hair," I shouted

back and slammed the door violently in his face. The nerve of him, treating me like a doormat when I was his wife.

I rushed into my walk-in closet to get ready, and to my surprise, red, white, and gold balloons danced around the room. These colors were special to me. They symbolized, our marriage as these were the colors we'd picked for our wedding. I danced along with them while I searched for an outfit, but I didn't have to look any further. It looked like Chase had bought something for me and wrapped it in a beautiful gold box tied with a red ribbon.

This was the Chase I had fallen in love with. Maybe this had all just been a game for my thirty-fourth birthday. I opened up the big box and found that it was pretty much empty. Exactly how I was beginning to feel. Pretty on the outside, but empty on the inside. In the box was an envelope, and in the envelope were divorce papers. I froze. The music seemed to fade. I staggered, and held a hand out to steady myself. When the tears began to flow I collapsed in the corner as the floodgates opened, releasing all of the anguish I had tried to suppress these past months.

Minutes later Zoe ran into the room. "Vanessa, where are you?" she shouted, all loud and obnoxious. "Are you ready?" She shut off the music and I could hear her searching for me. It wasn't long before she peeked into the closet, where I was balled up in a fetal position. She snatched the papers from my hand and after realizing what they were, and taking a few minutes to read through the details, she held me and cried with me. "It's okay. It's your birthday and guess what? WE can cry if we want to." She wiped the tears away, then reached into her bag and handed me a pen. "Sign them. Give him what he wants."

"I can't just sign it. I'm not ready."

"Well you better get ready. Because he's leaving the house to you and he's splitting all of the accounts with you, evenly."

Confused, I muttered, "Why though? I don't understand."

"Let me help you understand," she said. "You're going to be a millionaire. Happy birthday, bitch."

A divorce right now *felt* like it had come out of nowhere. Granted, our marriage was in trouble, but considering counseling first seemed a little more appropriate. As most divorces wouldn't go this smooth, I guess I had to not only accept it but also appreciate it. One thing is for sure, I wasn't signing those papers.

Playfully shaking me, Zoe continued, "Now don't keep me waiting. Get up and put some damn clothes on. Oh, and bring your bag. You're treating today 'cause you got the dough." Zoe always knew what buttons to push to lighten me up. I was thankful for her friendship. She was the sister I never had.

Once we were out, I found myself in a better mood, enjoying my life, if just for the moment. It felt like it was below zero degrees in New York, but my naturally curly hair kept me warm.

Christmas was just a week away, and every year it was our thing to visit Santa and sit on his lap. As we stood in line waiting, I realized I wanted to sit on this Santa's face because he was so damn fine. I whispered to Zoe, "Mmm, I would like to be his HoHoHo."

Zoe giggled, "Now that would be a December to remember. 'Tis the season to be giving, fa-la-la-la-la-la, la-la-la-la."

As we got to the front of the line, one of Santa's elves asked us, "Have you ladies been naughty or nice?"

Zoe replied, "Naughty is the new nice. Get with it."

When we finally got to Santa, he greeted us with a "Hohoho! Merry Christmas and a Happy New Year!" Then asked, "What can Santa do for you ladies this year?"

Zoe replied, "Well, I just want forgiveness from all of the wives of the married men I fucked. All of the homes I was a part of breaking up." She looked at me and continued, "I really am sorry." I didn't know what she wanted me to say, but embarrassment quickly took over that she would take it that far in front of a complete stranger. "Yeah, I guess that would be nice," Zoe said.

Zoe had a good heart, but it was a broken heart, and a broken heart can't love nobody. Since we were kids, I always tried to help her try to resolve her problems, but she was older now and stuck in her pain.

"And you, Vanessa? What can Santa do for you?" Santa asked.

"Love. Genuine love. I want to be loved again and I want to give love." Then I stopped in my tracks, confused. "Wait a minute," I said. "How'd you know that? How did you know my name?"

"Oh dear, Santa knows everybody's name."

Zoe was skeptical. "Yeah right. I stopped believing in Santa when my father died and I was forced to live with my mother and stepfather. But that's another story." Challenging him, she asked, "What's my name then?"

"I believe your name is Zoe."

If I didn't believe in Santa anymore, a small part of me definitely believed in him now. We took our pictures and Santa handed us a card that read, "If I can give you any gift, I'd give you love and laughter. Merry Christmas."

Walking away, Zoe shouted, "Girl! Santa was packing. Did you see that? Did you *feel* that?" Parents waiting on the line got mad and covered their kids' ears. Zoe didn't have a filter and her mouth always got us in trouble, even as children.

Just then, I looked across the mall and spotted two girls

that reminded me of Zoe and I back in the day. They were shopping, living life, and laughing while the boys around them were no doubt plotting on how to get them.

I pointed to them and said to Zoe, "Look at us all over again when we were younger." I couldn't help but notice that one of the girls did in fact look exactly like Zoe looked when we were their age.

Zoe got a faraway look in her eyes as she watched the girls, then quickly turned her attention back to me. "Nessa, I'm ready to get up out of here. It's your birthday, let's do something different." I took the cue to change the subject when I recognized Zoe's discomfort.

"Well I do have two tickets to poetry night at Club Vibes. We can just stick around for the poetry session and then leave."

"Oh yes, wherever the men are, you know I'm there."

CHAPTER 4

Vanessa, December 2012

Silence speaks when words can't. When bodies and souls can't. The connection turns into a disconnect. Physically you are here but mentally and emotionally you are somewhere else and that is not enough.

So, tell me, who is she? Why are you so checked out?

We are lying in this California king bed, where I once felt like your queen. You now have me feeling like a peasant. Our bodies are not even touching. You turn around and now I have your back to watch, and those welts are from someone else because my perfectly manicured nails haven't scratched into your skin in months.

Days turned into weeks. Weeks turned into months. But before these months make a year, I will leave you lying here alone and you won't even have my ass to kiss.

A round of applause broke out as I stood in the middle of a small yet intimate crowd of blurry faces I barely recognized—thanks to the Long Island Iced Tea I'd guzzled down minutes before hitting the stage. I'd come here once a month to perform a piece of my written work. This was my therapy, a creative outlet allowing me to vent to a group of strangers. The best part was that I wasn't judged.

My body felt warm from the buzz. It was as if everyone was painted in black and white. But sitting in the center of the room was a man so African and bold, he seemed to be the only body painted in color. He looked so familiar, so handsome, but I couldn't remember where I might have seen him before. All I knew was my pussy wanted to say hello. Well, she wanted to say hello to every man we encountered being that my husband was being "stingy with the dick," as Zoe would say.

I wanted to approach him, but I didn't know how. What would I say? *Hello, my name is Vanessa and I'm married, but I think you are really attractive?* Ugh that didn't sound right. The little voice in the back of my head said, Take your married ass home, and that is what I intended to do after finding Zoe.

I walked to the ladies' room. The liquor from earlier had made its way through my bloodstream and straight to my bladder. A fucking line, you have to be kidding me, I said to myself when I saw how many others were waiting. After five minutes, I approached the lady in the front of the line, and asked if I could go ahead of her because it was about to be an emergency for me. To my surprise she agreed to let me go— until every woman behind her started sucking their teeth and making nasty remarks.

One shouted in a grating voice, "If you let her skip, I'm skipping too!" Then everyone started verbally attacking her. At this point I was doing the pee-pee dance, but they didn't care.

Half of them were just as drunk as I was, or drunker, so I understood.

Across the way was the men's room. There was also a line, but it was definitely shorter. This time I decided I wasn't going to ask for permission to skip. I started making my way over when I heard the toilet flush, which I thought would be followed by the sound of the faucet running, but I guess the guy was too drunk to wash his hands and I was too drunk to care. The door flung open and I ran in before the next guy could make it. Voices from the line screamed, "C'mon!"

"Sorry guys!" I yelled back to them while locking the door.

Just my luck, the stall had an "out of order" sign on it but the urinal seemed to be working just fine. I pulled my Burgundy dress above my waist and my panties down to my ankles, and in my stilettos, I stood up strong and proud, urinating like a man, which felt pretty liberating. I must've been standing there for about a minute before the guy I jumped ahead of started banging on the door and hollering like he didn't have much sense. I wasn't about to waste my energy and breath on him.

I took my sweet time and when I was done I walked over to the mirror. I needed to freshen up. I pulled out my lipstick and leaned in to apply it. Seconds later, the stall door opened. I thought I was hallucinating so I continued applying my lipstick until a heavy-set man with dreads exited the stall and smacked my behind. "Nice ass, ma," he said.

I stood there shocked and embarrassed, but not as embarrassed as the woman in the stall who stood there fixing her skirt. Zoe. She looked at me and we both busted out in laughter.

"Girl, don't ask no questions. I'll tell you everything later."

"How am I the married one and can't get no dick, yet here you are?" I said with an attitude as I helped Zoe get herself together.

"You ain't the only one married around here," Zoe said looking at the guy, who was washing his hands at the sink.

He turned around and chimed in, "What y'all finna do tonight? We can go to my condo and have a little fun."

I almost threw up in my mouth. "Does anyone respect marriages around here?"

"Take your country ass home to your wife," Zoe yelled as she playfully pushed him out of the bathroom and locked the door.

"I thought we agreed: 'no more married men'," I said to her.

"Nessa, married men fuck better," she whined.

I could feel my facial expression change. An angry gaze came over my face that sliced right through her. "Zoe have you been drinking?"

Her bushy brows united in a frown. She hesitated a moment too long before replying, "Drinking what? Fucking GINGER ALE, yeah. I can't drink to keep me occupied so I have to fuck."

She rolled her eyes at me, but luckily, we were interrupted because I didn't have the patience to entertain Zoe and her scandalous behavior.

From the other side of the door, the guy who Zoe just fucked yelled, "Can I get your number, Destiny?" Destiny was the name Zoe gave to "just-for-the-moment" men. Hearing him call her that, I knew he was nothing special.

I cleared my throat and asked, "Well did he at least have a big dick?"

"Big and black," she replied, heading back into the bathroom stall to collect her long blonde wig, which she sometimes wore when we went out to cover her natural black hair. She loved getting into character and looking completely different when we went out. I felt like I had multiple best friends because with each look came a different personality.

Men never got bored with her, but she sure got bored with them. She couldn't keep a man because she couldn't keep her legs closed. Zoe was drop-dead gorgeous. She was the cream to my coffee, but she let every guy squirt their cream in her coffee. One thing she *was* strict about was condoms. She actually walked around with a box in her bag, which was a ho thing, but also a good thing since she was protecting herself, I guess.

Zoe ran back to the bathroom stall. This time it was to throw up. If the restroom really wasn't out of order, it would be now. We headed out of the restroom, ignoring the angry drunk men waiting in line.

"What's the plan after this?" asked Zoe.

"Maybe getting you home after all that puking," I suggested.

"I don't know about that. But I do know the night is still young and your outfit is too cute to go home so soon to a man that don't want you."

"Oh, well, thanks Zoe for making me feel good," I said sarcastically.

"I know what's going to make you feel good," Zoe said then turned to the bartender and shouted, "Jordan! One double shot of Hennessy." The bartender nodded at the request.

"And a ginger ale," I teased. It was really no fun drinking alone, but Zoe was naturally high on life and didn't need any substances to make her have a good time.

"One double shot of Hennessy and a ginger ale coming right up," he yelled back. Zoe knew Hennessy would make me either want to fight or fuck and fucking wasn't happening tonight.

Just then, I heard a disembodied voice say, "Do you really want to know who she is?"

At that moment, I felt like my heart had stopped beating as I stopped breathing. Zoe was too caught up flirting with the bartender and trying to get free shots to notice anything. I turned around, and there stood the man I was admiring a few minutes ago.

"Do I want to know who she is?" I repeated.

He came closer to me, and I could now feel him breathing on my neck. "Yes. The other woman. Do you really want to know who she is?"

Was there really another woman? I frantically elbowed Zoe to pass me my shot.

Like the life of the party Zoe screamed, "Yasssss bitch drink up, cheers to life." She turned around and we tossed our drinks back. Usually I would need a chaser, but I was thrown off as Zoe licked her lips and flirted with the guy standing in front of me.

"Oh wait! And who are you?"

I caught a whiff of alcohol on her breath. She had been lying to me the entire night. Sneaking drinks is childish, but this wasn't the place to scold her.

In a gruff voice he replied, "I'm Lance." He reached out

to shake my hand but I was too distracted by Zoe to acknowledge his pleasant gesture.

Zoe, on the other hand, swerved right in to grasp his masculine hand. "I'm Zoe," she said, then looked down at his fingers. "I see there's no wedding ring."

Just that quick she went from Destiny to Zoe. I guess she was feeling him because he looked like someone important. She whispered in my ear, "He looks like a walking dollar sign. Cha-Ching!"

His body language confirmed he was as annoyed with her as I was. "No offense, Zoe, but you're not my type."

She rolled her pretty chestnut eyes hard and she continued, "I guess married women are."

He then gave her a sly smile. "Maybe you and I have something in common then?"

Zoe was clearly upset but I was dying with laughter on the inside. In a confused and reckless manner, she grabbed her jacket. "I'm going out for some air," she said, and huffed away.

He unbuttoned his well fitted Black Armani vest and placed himself in the seat next to me. "Sometimes jealousy doesn't live far."

I didn't have to be a rocket scientist to know that he was talking about Zoe. "I don't know you well enough for you to be passing judgments on my friend."

He laughed at my comment then motioned to the bartender, who knew exactly what to make without asking. He then turned his attention back to me. "We have a habit of using the word 'friend' so loosely. Be careful. Everybody isn't your friend. Just because they hang around you and laugh with you doesn't mean they're for you."

"You're right. She's more like my sister and you're just a stranger."

"But we can change that title. Get to know me," he said.

I didn't expect for everyone to understand Zoe. She was definitely complicated, but her present and her future were a result of her past. I always had her back, no matter what, because I knew where she came from and what she been through.

My husband was another one that didn't think much of Zoe. He had only met her once -- at our wedding. She was only there briefly because she was filming for her first feature film and had to rush back to Los Angeles. Zoe left a bad taste in his mouth, though. Chase always asked to see this special film that was so important and to think about it, I've never seen it either. Chase always warned me to stay away from her, but I ignored him just like I was ignoring this guy sitting next to me.

"It's funny," I said. "People breeze into your life and want to tell you how to run shit."

"You're stubborn. I like that."

The bartender brought over two glasses of water with a lemon wedge in it. *What kind of cheap man is this?* I thought to myself, *I'm sitting at a bar and he buys me a water?* I'm not a gold digger, but I could honestly have bought this myself.

As if he had read my mind, he explained, "I ordered you a glass of water because you look like you may have already had too much to drink tonight."

He was right. I felt dehydrated and like I might pass out sooner rather than later. I was feeling him a lot more, and now he had my full attention. He looked a lot more attractive, a lot more intelligent, and not to mention, he looked like a boss. Or maybe it was the liquor. I was already in the exciting stage of being drunk. You know, the "hook-up" stage, where everyone in the bar starts looking attractive.

"It's about three hours to sunrise," he said, looking at the bar clock, "let me drive you home"

I wanted to accept his offer because neither Zoe or I drove when we went out on nights like this, but I declined. "I wouldn't want to disrespect my husband. I'll order an Uber." I paused before asking, "So what if I really wanted to know who she is?"

There was an awkward silence. He cleared his throat. "You should never ask a man who the other woman is unless you're prepared to walk away from him."

"And if I stay?"

He squeezed his lemon into his water and continued, "Then you're know different than the other woman."

Wow, I thought. "So I let him cheat in peace?"

"Now that's for you to decide, but a woman's intuition is always right. You don't have to stay," he told me.

"Well, I guess I can't control who I attract."

"But you can control what you accept."

Oh my God, my drunken booming mind thought. *Married or not, this man can get the pussy right here, right now, on top of the bar while everyone watches.*

As Zoe stumbled back to us Lance politely got up, buttoned his vest, leaned in, and whispered, "Just remember, some people come into our lives with ulterior motives and hidden agendas. Goodnight, beautiful."

The fine hairs on my neck stood at attention because of the chills he gave me. He walked over to the bartender, Jordan, and whispered something that caused them both to look in my direction.

"Jordan, what's the tab?" I yelled. "I'm getting out of here."

Zoe sat down and in an unfashionable manner and put her hand under her chin. "So what's his deal?"

Jordan smiled at us then walked over and presented us

with two more bottles of water. "Detective Jennings took care of the tab, ladies. Be safe."

Zoe got all excited and looked around. "Girl, he can lock me up and throw away the fucking key. I'm gonna get him. Wait and see. He's just playing hard to get, that's all."

Zoe could never take rejection, and she always broke the girlfriend code. Even Stevie Wonder could have seen that Lance and I had been digging each other.

I gave her the benefit of the doubt, per usual. But I had a few words for her. "Remind me not to hang out with you during the next few months. It's really shameful I have to babysit a grown ass woman."

She snapped, "What did you want me to do Nessa. It's tempting as a mother fucker. I tried to not drink for the night but look the fuck around, everybody is drinking."

"You're old enough. You know right from wrong. I'm tired of making excuses for you. It's not about you anymore." My hand wandered to her stomach and she slapped it away.

"I'm sorry Nessa, we should have just left when you mentioned it earlier. Are you happy now?"

"No, I'm sorry. I should never have trusted you to keep your promise. I knew that by the end of the night I'd regret bringing you here."

I was distracted from our conversation by something shining beside me. A 14-karat, two-row diamond bracelet sat on the bar where Lance had just been seated. It must have slipped off his wrist. I picked it up in a hurry before anyone else could see.

"O-M-G let's keep it and pawn it," Zoe begged.

"That wouldn't be the right thing to do and you know it."

"That's an easy fifty grand, Nessa! You don't need the money, but I can use it for the baby. Please."

I fixed her with a steady look. "I promised you that the baby would never want for anything. Unlike you, I keep my promises." I got up and made my way through the small crowd, screaming Lance's name in a whisper, trying not to cause a scene. Zoe tagged along behind me like a puppy, trying to get me to change my mind.

When I raced outside the club, the winter air smacked me in my face. My hair was blown and tossed in every direction. The weather was just as cold and angry as my failing marriage, and I threw my fur poncho across my shoulders for warmth and protection.

I spotted Lance, who was already halfway down the block. "Mr. Jennings? Mr. Jennings!" I screamed, but I guess not loudly enough. He continued opening the door to a black BMW.

The bouncer, Dan, was standing at the door. He saw what was going on, and whistled once, through his fingers.

That got Lance's attention, and he looked over his shoulder at us. He saw us flagging him down, and headed our way. He and I walked towards each other, meeting in the middle. "Thank you," I called to Dan. "I owe you one!"

"Don't mention it, Nessa. You know you fam."

Lance approached me. "Did you want that ride home?"

"No, you actually left something at the bar."

"Yeah, I know."

"You know?" I asked. My mind was racing. Was this a setup? Was he waiting to see if I'd return his bracelet to see if he could trust me?

His cold hands touched my cheeks. "I left the most gorgeous woman I've ever seen in my life."

The only thing I could do at this point was blush. My rose-petal lips cracked a smile, then I laughed. He was very charming. I grabbed his hand, touching his wrist. "Your wrist. It's naked." I took the bracelet out of my coat pocket and placed it in his hand. "I'll see you around."

CHAPTER 5

Vanessa, May 2013

Six Months Later - Present Day

Gently placing my ear against the white bathroom door, I heard Chase whispering. I guessed he must've been on the phone with someone. The sound of the water from the shower drowned out his voice, so I couldn't understand a word he was saying.

After a few seconds of standing there, I started obnoxiously knocking and shouted, "Hey, I'm making a grocery run. Do you need anything?" Clearly a lie, as I was standing there in my black satin robe with nothing on underneath. My intent was for that bitch on the other end of the phone to hear me loud and clear.

His whispers and the running water came to an abrupt stop. When he walked out of the bathroom fully clothed, it threw me for a loop as I was expecting him to be covered in a towel and smelling fresh, like Dove soap. As he walked passed me, the mild musk of his scent was rich in the air.

He still looked rattled from an argument we'd had earlier that morning when I did the walk of shame. We didn't argue about my whereabouts. We argued because he didn't ask about my whereabouts. I didn't understand how I had been out all night with another man and it didn't even bother him. How was he so oblivious? It was like Chase knew another man had me but didn't care.

His voice was soft, "I ran you a bath. I'll be home a little late so don't wait up." He must've known my anxiety was through the roof and a hot bath was the only way to calm me. And to wash another man off of me. He looked like he needed that bath more than I did. He kissed me on my forehead like I was a child instead of kissing me passionately like I was his wife, and he left.

A few months ago, I probably would have gotten into my car to follow him but I couldn't stop thinking about my morning with Lance. I decided to stay optimistic and texted the one person I knew could turn my day around: *Come over. I moved the key. It's under the flowerpot to the right of the mailbox. Chase will be gone all day.*

I walked into the steamy bathroom. I wiped the fog off of the mirror and took a minute to admire my body as I slowly undressed. I didn't know what Chase saw when he looked at me, but my eyes witnessed art. *One man's loss is definitely another man's gain.* As I stepped into the tub, the water that engulfed my hourglass figure did nothing to calm the pleasure urges that consumed me. My hands slow danced around my body and stopped when they found their destination. But thrusting a finger inside of my pussy wasn't enough. I craved something more, something bigger, something real. Deep in my imagination, I felt a cold shock run up my spine, making me clench my butt cheeks.

I opened my eyes and there he stood in the doorway. All I could see through the thick steam in the room was a silhouette of a tall, dark, masculine man. I lusted over him as the water licked my hard nipples ever so gently, and wished it was his tongue on me instead.

I stood there, inviting him in to join me. He turned off the light switch, I guess to be romantic but all I seen was teeth and eyeballs. Impatiently he pushed himself against me while positioning his hands on my hips. I reached for his dick, but he pulled back, making me beg for it.

Water dripped down my ass, making it moist enough for him to enter as he pushed my face against the wall. Lance grabbed my hair, yanking my head back. I moaned in lust, screaming breathlessly and biting down on my bottom lip. He pulled even harder. I was feeling that shit until I heard my track snatch. It didn't even matter. He could have snatched me until I was bald. It was the pain that I needed and the connection to a man's soul. I wanted to feel the pulse of him create pain until heat punched through my pelvis.

He positioned me on all fours. My ass raised, jiggling like a dog who was happy to see her owner. He gripped my ass cheeks just to spread them apart so that he could eat my ass like the groceries I lied about getting this morning. I was lost in a fog of sexual gratification as he gently applied kisses, sliding his tongue in and out of my ass while fingering my vagina. It felt all too good.

"Sit on my face," he commanded. Without hesitation, I did just as he told me. I strapped my legs around his head, maneuvering my waist as my hips gyrated on his face. He fucked me with his warm lips and wet tongue as he continued slapping and squeezing my ass.

"Yes, Daddy!" The more I called him Daddy, the deeper his tongue went, and the more he slurped and ate. I was almost at that point of explosion when I was startled by the sound of a bell.

I opened my eyes and quickly shut them, hoping to continue this dream, which felt more like the reality I had experienced earlier that morning with Lance. I couldn't see much in the dark room but the time on the wall read six-oh-nine, which reminded me of the sixty-nine position that was about to go down as I daydreamed.

Feeling guilty, I stumbled out of the tub, and my bare feet slipped on the wet marble floor. My body clenched as it hit the ground. Quickly recovering, I stood up and wrapped myself in my robe.

Water was still glistening on my body when Zoe entered with a bottle of champagne. I could see attitude written all over her face, as if I'd done something wrong. Barging right in to escape the sun, she babbled, "What took you so long? I was about to leave!" She dropped her purse in the foyer and continued wobbling into the living room, unsnapping her bra as she walked.

"Why didn't you use the key?"

"What key?"

"Didn't I text you where the key was and you replied 'okay'?"

She whipped her bra through her sleeve and tossed it over the arm of the couch. Plopping into the seat with exhaustion, she said, "Oh shit girl... you right. But you know I suffer from short-term memory loss."

It was true. Zoe's memory had started getting bad, but I assumed it was just from the pregnancy.

"You forget everything else except for that damn bottle."

Now she laughed. Thank God that lightened the mood. I didn't need any more bad energy around me or I would have kicked her ass out myself, pregnant or not.

The champagne cork popping was like listening to my favorite choir at church on a Sunday morning. Of course, Zoe couldn't drink so I grabbed only one champagne flute from the kitchen and got her a glass of water before heading back to the living room. Watching the drink spill into my glass and seeing the golden bubbles swirl around gave me good vibes.

I could tell Zoe's mouth was watering, but I had to remind her, "One more month." After settling down we raised our glasses and we clinked them together. "Cheers to twenty-five years of friendship and to the ninety-nine years to come," I toasted.

The champagne had an underlying taste of peach. It was everything I needed but I hadn't eaten all day. "I have to eat something before I have another drink," I told her. Drinking on an empty stomach was never a good idea for me.

"I came over because I thought you were cooking," she said over her glass.

"Cooking? I'm not doing any domestic chores around here. I'm on strike."

Picking up my wedding picture from the end table, she spoke with a reminiscing tone. "Y'all was so happy," she said. "How'd that change so fast?"

I just sat there and shook my head. I didn't have an answer.

"You see, this is exactly why I'm not getting married," she said, then added, smugly, "and you should have listened to me when I told you not to get married."

I have always tried to get Zoe to settle down and she has always tried to get me to explore dicks and "live life," as she says.

"Marriage, I think, is one of the most beautiful concepts

there is and I'm glad I didn't listen to you because it was a good experience."

"There's no such thing as happily ever after, Nessa. I mean, look at you now."

I snatched my wedding picture from her. "It doesn't always work out, but there's always light at the end of the tunnel. Whether you walk through that tunnel alone or with someone."

"Well, I don't want to get married."

Annoyed with her, I continued, "Of course you don't want to get married. You just want to fuck married men."

"Well, why be committed to one man when you can have options?"

"Because being wanted by every man doesn't compare to being valued by one man."

"To each her own, Nessa." Zoe always threw shade, even on a sunny day. I was starting to realize maybe my husband and Lance were right when they preached about not liking the company I kept.

I ignored her. "Anyway, I guess somebody else has his attention now. But it's cool, because somebody else has my attention too."

With a burst of excitement Zoe screamed, "What, bitch? Tell me more! I wanna know everything."

I didn't want to get into the details with Zoe because I knew she had a little lingering crush on Lance from that night we first met him at the bar. She knew we had been casually speaking, but didn't think it was anything serious. I decided to distract her by telling her we'd talk about it over dinner. She agreed and we headed to the kitchen. "Let's see what you have in here," Zoe said as she looked through my cabinets. "You don't have shit," she said. "What did you go to the supermarket for?"

Why did she think I went to the supermarket? Unless...? Chase and Zoe...? No, that couldn't be. But when she smiled sarcastically, I wasn't sure. I put down my drink and folded my arms across my chest. Staring at her coldly, I asked, "What makes you think I went to the supermarket, Zoe?"

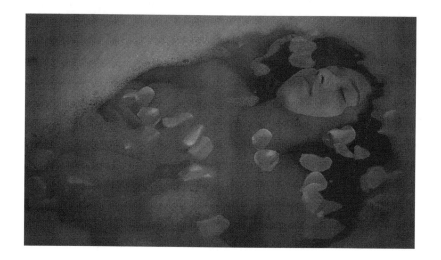

CHAPTER 6

Chase, September 2012

There was a day back in September of 2012 that I will forever regret. It was the day that changed my life.

I sat in a pub waiting for Abraham to arrive after his shift. He was an FBI agent, but he was also my lifelong best friend. As boys, he wanted to be a surgeon and I wanted to be a police officer. Funny how everything worked out. We met at this pub every Tuesday night to either celebrate life or mourn it.

I was feeling broken because of a surgery I had performed that day. It didn't start or end well. "Ma'am there's only a twenty percent chance we'll be able to save your daughter," I had told my patient's mother as tears poured out of her, along with her heart.

"Just do it, please. I trust you. They say you're the best doctor in New York."

People didn't understand that I was just a doctor. I wasn't God. They expected me to bring the dead back to life. Sometimes I just couldn't do it.

"I don't recommend you do this surgery. There's an 80

percent chance your daughter won't survive."

She fell to her knees and begged me to do the surgery and I begged her not to go through with it, but she signed those papers. Basically signing her daughter's death certificate.

"I knew there was no way she would make it out of that surgery alive. She should have listened to me, god dammit." I banged my hand on the bar top, resulting in a sharp pain.

"Stop overthinking everything," Abraham told me when I shared the story with him. "You did what you could do and now you have to move on. It's life, man. Some things are out of our control." He was right, but it was easier said than done. He picked at my hair. "I see one, two, three grays. Keep stressing and you'll have a whole head full of them."

We both laughed, tossed back our shots, and stared straight ahead. "I wonder if her mother still thinks I'm the best surgeon in New York. Between me and you, deep down I actually thought I could save her." I shook my head in disbelief.

"Please don't forget all the good you've done. Don't forget about all of the successful surgeries you've performed. You've saved so many lives, Chase," Abraham said, trying to make me feel better. But nothing was working.

I didn't have anything to offer, so Abraham talked about his day. "I had a tough day too, for what it's worth. I had to defuse a bomb in an elementary school." He shook his head and continued his report to me. "In a school, man. Innocent children almost died. I almost lost my life. My unborn son was seconds away from being fatherless."

"Vanessa wants children so bad, especially now that Jordy is pregnant. But I don't know if I'm ready."

"What! I thought you were ready?"

"I mean, look at my patient's family. Now they have to plan a funeral. No parents should ever have to bury their child. Doesn't that frighten you?"

"Honestly, if I thought about all of the bad shit that could possibly happen in life, I wouldn't be living my best life and that wouldn't be fair to me. The only thing you can do is develop healthy affirmations, speak that shit into existence, and pray my brother."

I patted Abraham on the back. "You're a hero, man. I'm proud of what you did today."

"We're both heroes."

"I sure don't feel like it."

"Heroes don't win every battle, Chase. That's what you have to understand."

I didn't like drinking, but that night I was going to drink until the pain went away. "Another round," I shouted at the bartender.

Abraham got up from the bar. "I have bigger battles on my hands," he explained. "I'm in the dog house. I'm trying to get home early tonight, you know, to be a good boy."

"She called off the wedding, didn't she?"

"Yup, and it's not from cold feet either."

Around that time, two casually dressed women entered the bar and walked over to Abraham. "Is this seat taken?" one of them asked.

"No, I was just leaving," he said.

One of the ladies looked vaguely familiar to me but I couldn't place where I might know her from. A patient's family member perhaps? I couldn't think about patients any more tonight. I was already feeling my liquor and didn't want to think about anything else. She softly spoke to Abraham. "Are you leaving your friend here for us?"

He looked in my direction. "My friend is leaving too, right?"

"No. I think I may stay a little longer. How about one more shot before you go?"

"Nah, you finish that up and go home so you don't end up in the dog house like me." We hugged and Abraham took off.

The women started conversing with me. "So, are you going to buy us a drink or are you just going to let us sit here parched?"

The sober me would have ignored them. Instead, I engaged them with. "Am I going to get a name?"

The friend with the long blonde hair and brown skin reached over to shake my hand. "I'm Destiny, and this is my friend, Belle."

"You look a little familiar, Destiny, though I'm not sure where I know you from."

She licked her polished lips and continued, "Well, what's your name? Maybe I can tell you where you know me from."

"I thought you already knew his name," Belle chimed in.

Destiny stuttered a little and quickly explained, "I told my friend over here that you looked familiar but I don't know from where. Is your name Steven?"

I laughed because Steven was Vanessa's ex-boyfriend's name. Actually, he was her first love and it took her a while to get over him. "My name is Chase. It's nice to meet you."

Out of nowhere the other woman snapped, "This isn't right," and took off.

"What's up with her?"

"Just a bad day, I guess," Destiny said, once Belle was gone.

"I know about bad days a little too well," I replied.

She rubbed my hand. "Well, that's one less person you have to buy a drink for."

We sat at the bar for hours and what started out as innocent conversation ended up with the both of us stumbling out of the bar.

I searched for my keys but couldn't find them. Destiny began stroking her hands up and down my arm. I instantly pulled away.

"I insist," she said. "Let me help you find your keys." She walked in front of me and knelt down while frisking me. She looked up at me, her eyes sparkling. "I didn't find your keys but I found something else."

A feeling of euphoria took over me, unleashing an arousal I was trying to control.

"Can I touch you here?" she asked.

Nervously I stepped back. "No, no, no! You can't do that. Might not be a good idea." I waved my hand in the air showing her my wedding ring and thank God, she backed off.

"I have a little secret," she whispered in my ear. "Your friend took your keys."

Embarrassed because I had no way of getting home or getting into my home, I called Abraham. As it was three in the morning, it went right to his voicemail. Waving the phone in disappointment I mumbled, "He don't quite agree with drinking and driving. Plus he's in law enforcement."

She quietly giggled. "That makes sense. Why don't you let me take you home? I don't mind."

"Knowing my friend, he probably got me a room next door at the Marriott."

"Seems like a routine," she said.

I felt a vibration coming from my coat pocket. To my surprise, I saw it was Vanessa calling and I tried to sober up as fast as possible.

"Hi baby, what are you doing up?"

"I was calling to make sure you got in safe."

"Yeah, yeah, I was actually looking for my keys but..."

She cut me off mid-sentence. "But Abraham took them because you had too much to drink tonight. And he told me why. I'm sorry that happened to you today."

I exhaled, feeling relieved. "Of course he told you."

"Of course he did. Now go next door and get some sleep. He'll be there in the morning to pick you up."

"Okay, I miss you already."

"I miss you too. Two weeks down," she said.

"Two more to go."

"Well about that, I was going to fly to Baltimore after

this to see my parents. So it'll be more like three to four weeks to go. Are you okay with that?"

"You're killing me, Vanessa. But I think that's a good idea."

Vanessa spoke softly as she changed the subject, "Chase, as doctors we try our hardest to save everyone. If we could, we would trade our own lives for theirs. Sadly, it doesn't quite work that way. Some things we just can't control."

"I know, baby."

"I love you, Chase. Get some rest."

Just as I hung up the call from my wife, Destiny fell to the pavement. It seems she had too much to drink. Blood gushing from her knee sent her into a panic. Trying to be a hero for the second time today, I raced over to her.

"Oh God, I need to go to the hospital. There's blood everywhere. It hurts so bad I can't even walk." From the look of it, she was pretty badly bruised.

"I'm a doctor. If you come upstairs with me I can clean it up, but I can't promise that the pain will instantly go away."

She agreed, and I carried her up to the executive suite at the Marriot. After cleaning her cut and carefully wrapping it up, Destiny fell asleep. I decided to let her stay. After all, we would be sleeping in two separate rooms. She was a fine woman, but not at all my type.

I decided to take a shower and then call it a night, but when I stepped out of the bathroom, I was greeted by Destiny, laid out on my bed and partially exposed as a fishnet bodysuit tightly hugged her curves. She urgently began rubbing her clit and the battle between who I needed and who I wanted took action. I needed my wife, but in this moment I wanted Destiny. I closed my eyes and opened them. This was not a dream.

"Come here. I wanna make you feel good."

I was at once skeptical and intrigued. She danced her way to me, "Don't be nervous Chase."

I was on edge. This was the first time I cheated on Vanessa. I knew it wasn't worth it but the tingle she sent through my soul as she licked drops of water from my body made me want more, so I allowed her to take over. She sucked me until my eyes rolled to the back of my head. I picked her up and tossed her petite body on to the white sheets. After crawling on top of her I realized, "Shit we don't have a condom."

"I think I have one in my bag." She ran out of the room and came back empty handed. "I'm all out," she said, following that quickly with, "Don't judge me. I'm a single woman looking for love."

It didn't even matter because after that night I knew I wouldn't see her for the rest of my life. I pushed her legs open and began punching and banging like a drum. Then she screamed out my name and I screamed out hers and it was over.

I fell asleep on the couch and let Destiny sleep in the room.

The next morning I was awakened by Abraham, sitting directly across from me with the newspaper in one hand and coffee in the other. The sun beaming through the window didn't help my hangover. The room looked immaculate, as if nothing ever happened. It made me wonder if I was dreaming as Destiny was gone, like she never existed.

Abraham cleared his throat. "Good morning," he said. "Do you want to explain what a pair of ladies' underwear is doing in this room?"

CHAPTER 7

Chase, October 2012

One Month Later

My hands were trembling as the blood from the chest wound ran straight to my fingertips. It seems as if the walls were caving in on me as I diverted my eyes to the long thin telescope that I clenched tightly in my left hand. Only my hands started to grow numb as I prepared to make half-inch incisions between my patient's ribs.

To slowly tread through the arteries and veins going into her injured heart I needed steady hands that I didn't have. I have trained medical students early on in their surgical rotations to hover the hand at stillness. Yet, the perfect doctor couldn't practice what he preached.

The tremor in my hand was a slight earthquake causing my world to collapse. Something didn't feel right. Maybe it was the guilt from my meaningless affair. Maybe it was the guilt from losing life on this same operating table in this same operating room. Standing in the chilled operating room seemed more like I was in a third-world country as my O.R. was rushed by a number of surgeons I had once trained.

After the surgery, I noticed Ms. Williams, who sat on

the hospital's board of directors standing by the door. Her eyes pierced through my soul, but when she said, "Dr. Moretti please come with me," my stomach was in knots.

Anger was the only emotion I felt as I was escorted from a successful surgery. I shadowed behind Ms. Williams, trying to avoid making a scene.

"I demand to know what this is about," I told her in a loud whisper. "I provide patients with the best possible surgical care, I don't agree with being interrupted before, during, or after surgery like this."

She continued to walk a few steps ahead of me. "It is a private matter. We will discuss it in private." It was at that moment we got into the elevator I realized my life was about to go down as fast as the elevator ride. I didn't quite comprehend what was happening, but the silence and her facial expression told me it was more serious than I could have imagined. While I felt the weight of the world on my shoulders, I had to force myself to smile and be polite each time others entered or exited the elevator.

The conference room she took me to was empty and cold. "Dr. Moretti, please have a seat," she instructed.

"I'd rather stand, if that's okay with you," I respectfully replied.

Ms. Williams walked over and pulled a seat out from the table. "Dr. Moretti, please have a seat. I insist."

With some hesitation, I finally dropped into the chair and waited for her to break the awkward silence. While I waited, anxious, sweat rushed down my face. I grabbed a tissue from the table and patted my face dry. I let out a dry cough. "Why am I here?"

"Dr. Moretti, you are one of the top surgeons in New York, and I apologize but I can explain." I folded my arms across my chest and listened. "Your health has become a major concern," she began.

I jumped out of my seat. Resting my hands on the table I leaned forward. "If this is about the flu, you shouldn't worry because it's gone. Now please allow me to get back to work." I felt broken. Deep down inside my heart, I knew what was coming next. I had been having symptoms I was trying to suppress, but they couldn't be ignored for too long.

"Dr. Moretti, it's not about the flu. Please come back and have a seat."

I stopped right there and looked up at the ceiling to prevent the tears from falling. She didn't have to tell me anything else.

"The blood work you provided us with for our yearly testing indicates that you are in the acute HIV infection stage." I kept my back to her as I listened. I felt like I was being stabbed. "The flu you had is a symptom of seroconversion, which occurs in up to eighty percent of people infected." She couldn't stop talking for just a second to let me soak it all in,

"The good news is that your C.D. Four count is above a five hundred, which--"

"The good news? The good news? What is so good about this news? Tell me!" I shouted at her.

She continued. "Your count is above five hundred, which puts you in the percentage of good health. In order to keep you in this bracket we have to get you on treatment right away or else your count will drop."

The pain was palatable. I stood there in a daze, blocking all the noise, only thinking about my wife. I panicked. "No, that is a damn lie," I said, turning to face her. "You repeat those tests today and I mean it! It has to be a laboratory error. It has to be." My recent lack of sleep and the mountains of stress from the night sweats and the rapid weight loss were now starting to make sense. I knew it wasn't an error. I just prayed that it was.

"Yes, Dr. Moretti, I can definitely repeat the test. But in the meantime, we must follow the hospital's guideline to temporarily suspend your practice to keep your patients safe from risk. And we have to give you some time to mentally accept what's going on." She motioned for me to sit down. This time I did. When I was seated, she said, in a low, worried tone, "Can we talk about next steps, please?"

The tears wouldn't stop. Who ever said men don't cry lied -- I was broken. Physically, mentally, and emotionally. My heart was broken in a way that couldn't be surgically fixed. I suppose at some phase all of our hearts, including mine, will stop. I just didn't want to think about that now.

"Listen, you and I both know this is a manageable disease. It isn't the end of anything, just the beginning of living a more informed and conscious life. Trust me, I know," she said. I held my head in the palm of my hand as she comforted me. "It's okay to cry. These tears let us know we are human. I know what you're feeling."

"No, you don't," I snapped back. "I was supposed to give her kids. We planned on starting soon."

Sympathy was all over Ms. Williams face but I didn't need anyone to feel sorry for me. "Dr. Moretti I am so--"

I instantly cut her off again. "Please don't."

She nodded then told me, "I'm going to give you a minute." She lifted the jug of water on the table and poured a glass. "Well, it looks like it isn't cold enough," she said. "I'll go get us some fresh water." Before leaving, she paused then quietly spoke again. "And ummmm...Dr. Moretti. There's another file underneath yours with some valuable information that may ease your mind. But I didn't tell you it was there. Listen, I know you're a good man and you'll do the right thing."

The file underneath mine read "Vanessa Moretti." A person's information was to be confidential, no matter the relationship or results. My eyes quickly scanned the paper for her results. The results showed her to be negative for HIV. I had already known her status because I hadn't slept with her since she had been away for a month. Somehow, I couldn't stop thanking God for saving her, but cursing him for killing me.

As doctors, we are trained to break bad news all day to our patients and their families. We tell them we are sorry for their losses. We encourage them to be strong, to grieve, and move on. When it hits so close to home, when it's your back against the wall, it isn't that easy. In that moment, my soul died. The only thing worse than being close to death is losing your soul while you are still alive.

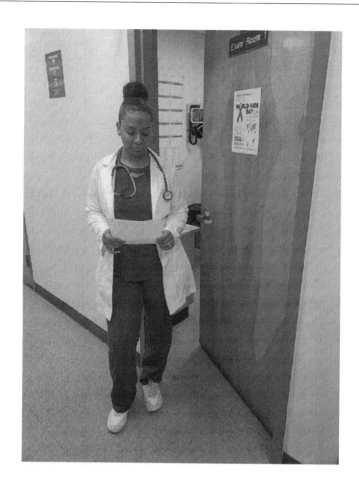

CHAPTER 8
Chase, October 2012

I left that meeting walking along the path of darkness. After hearing my death sentence, my chest felt tight, making it difficult to breathe. However, inhaling the warm autumn breeze seemed to help me relax. The sun had set, leaving the moon and the stars for my only company. Ten minutes had gone by, but it seemed like hours. Sitting in my SUV, I finally found the motivation to try to drive, until nausea took over. I quickly opened the door, leaned out, and let everything I had eaten that day rush from my stomach.

Riding home in silence, I thought about driving off a bridge and into the ocean. The only thing that stopped me was Vanessa. She didn't deserve that. She didn't deserve any of this. As I arrived at the house, Vanessa was pulling out of the driveway. When she spotted me, she immediately stopped her car and started walking towards me, smiling from ear to ear and eagerly waving to get my attention.

I felt frozen. Simple minded. Unable to think clearly about the picture-perfect life I had destroyed. I got out of my car to greet her and she wrapped her arms tightly around my neck. "Oh Chase, I missed you," she said. "This was the longest month ever." Despite the negative thoughts running through my head and the flutters in my stomach that made me sick, I took advantage of this moment, holding her as long as she would allow.

Vanessa knew me like the back of her hand. Pulling away, she squinted at me, trying to figure me out. "What's wrong?" she asked. "You know you can talk to me about anything."

I playfully grabbed her and pulled her back into my arms. "It's just work, but let's not talk about that."

"Well, I think you need a little distraction," she said, flirting. "Let's talk about that."

Clearing my throat, I declined her offer. "Not tonight, maybe tomorrow."

She pulled out of my arms and held my hands. "You know what, Chase? We can't save every life. And as much as I hate when you have these moments, I have to admire it, because it says a lot about your character. You're a good man and God knows your heart."

I was trying to escape making eye contact when she grabbed my cheeks and went in for a kiss. "But guess what? I know your heart too and I know something is not sitting well in there. When you're ready to talk to me, I'm here."

Her voice so angelic. Her touch so gentle, and her heart so pure. I was staring at the picture of perfection. In my eyes, she could do no wrong. She was still talking, "I thought you'd be at the hospital all night so I already made plans with Zoe."

Dumbfounded I asked, "Didn't she fly back to LA?"

"She decided to stay in New York a little longer. Said she has some good news or something, so I'm letting her stay at the beach house. I hope you don't mind?"

"Not at all. That's perfect. Now we have someone house sitting."

"She's in the car. Maybe you can be nice and say hello."

As much as I disliked Zoe, Vanessa loved her. I couldn't figure out why to save my life, but I decided, all things considered, I could give her a chance. What did I really know about her anyway? I'd only really met her once, briefly at our wedding, and after all, Vanessa will need her by her side when I tell her my secrets.

Zoe began beeping the horn of Vanessa's car, which pierced through my ears. But that wasn't the worst part.

I felt like I was hallucinating when Zoe rolled down her car window and there was Destiny sitting in the driver's seat. She waved at me and blew a kiss in my direction. My pulse surged beneath my skin and my legs began shaking with rage. I approached the vehicle and said in an angry whisper, "What are you doing with my wife?"

She got a malicious grin on her face. "Don't worry, Chase. Your secrets are safe with me."

I raised my voice and took on an aggressive tone, "You need to leave now," I told her, as Vanessa stood by me, horrified.

"Chase! What is your problem?"

I instantly realized I needed to somehow put a twist on this or Vanessa would suspect something. "I'm so sorry," I said, backtracking. "I, uh, thought she was someone else."

"Well she isn't someone else, Chase. She's Zoe, my best friend, and you need to chill out."

Then Zoe chimed in, "Well, technically, tonight I am someone else." She attempted to fix her wig and said with a smirk, "I'm Destiny."

Vanessa was angry but the face she made was not for Destiny, it was for me. Before walking away, she shook her head at me and said, "You are really becoming a different person. It's like I don't know you anymore. I think you need to learn how to separate work from your personal life."

I didn't know what to say. I was dumbstruck trying to process that Destiny was Zoe. That Zoe was Destiny. That I had sex with my wife's best friend, and that I was given a virus I couldn't cure.

It was as if karma the bitch herself had made a conscious decision to screw up my life. Foolish of me to ever have doubted the idea that what goes around comes around. Karma had it in for me, big time. I started to feel as if I was being punished by Satan himself, that there was a little red man sitting on my shoulder plotting to ruin my future. But for me, there was no future. Just a black hole.

Once upon a time, walking into my home had brought me such comfort but that wasn't the case today. I paced back and forth trying to make sense of it all but I couldn't. I called Vanessa's phone several times but was sent to voicemail. I was hoping Destiny -- I mean *Zoe* -- hadn't told her anything. I couldn't keep my eyes off of the door as I sat at the bar in my home, impatiently waiting to hear her keys in the lock. I poured drink after drink, desperate to see the woman I loved walk through the door. Praying she wouldn't come home broken.

I couldn't tell you how long I sat there drowning in my sorrows before my cell phone rang. I unsteadily ran to find it, spilling the wine in the glass I had just refilled, thinking it was going to definitely leave a stain on our white carpet. When I got to the phone I was disappointed. It wasn't Vanessa calling. It was Abraham, and I ignored the call.

A short time later, the doorbell started ringing nonstop. I dragged my body to the door, not surprised at all to see Abraham standing there.

"Damn, man. You look like you been through hell and back," he said.

"That's what I feel like."

As he came in, he continued, "I haven't seen you like this since med school. Talk to me, man."

I was dying inside. I needed an outlet. I needed to tell my truths to someone who wouldn't judge me. I wanted to pour it all out but how could I? As I stood there contemplating things, I decided that Abraham knew all of my secrets and this was just another one he'd take to the grave with him.

Once I'd told him everything, he was ready to take matters into his own hands. "It's a violation of the law to have unprotected sex while HIV positive," he told me, angrily. "We can put this bitch away for a long time."

"I know, but I can't do anything yet," I said. "I have to find a way to tell Vanessa first. I don't know how to tell her." Admitting my infidelity to my wife was definitely a conversation I wished I could avoid.

"The sooner she knows, the better. You have to tell her."

"There is little to no chance that we will recover from this and I don't know if I'm ready for a divorce."

"As men, we make mistakes. You made the deliberate decision to be with another woman and it was a big mistake, but it doesn't define you. What you do after this does."

"Crazy how one mistake could change my life forever."

"We are always one decision away from a better life or a life filled with regrets. Sorry it had to end like this man."

Vanessa finally came home. I thought she would be upset about me snapping at her friend earlier but instead she was excited. She greeted Abraham with a hug and then came over to kiss me. "You guys, I have good news. You won't believe what it is."

Thank God, she had some good news because I needed to hear something positive. "What is it?" I asked.

Jumping up and down like a kid in a candy store, she said, "Guess! You have to guess!" Before I could guess she blurted out, "Okay you guys are taking too long. Zoe is pregnant and I'm going to be a godmother."

CHAPTER 9
Chase, October 2012

My lungs felt like they were shutting down. Like there wasn't enough oxygen in the room and I was suffocating. Every muscle in my body felt like it had abandoned me. I couldn't move; I was paralyzed. I could see Vanessa's mouth moving with excitement but her voice was becoming distant.

Abraham walked over to me, his face full of worry. A while after, everything around me was starting to blur. My unfaithful heart began to beat uncontrollably. I tried to inhale deeply and exhale, warding off what was probably just a panic attack, but I felt seconds away from having a heart attack. I felt like I was dreaming until reality set in and Abraham brought me a glass of water. Vanessa was filled with too much joy to notice anything.

"How the fuck could this happen?" I asked Abraham, under my breath. "What the fuck am I going to do?"

"Well we know *how* it happened, man. Now what you're going to do is totally up to you."

We both stayed there stuck in a daze while Vanessa rambled on about being a godmother and how much she is going to enjoy spoiling the baby. My mind was working overtime thinking of a million ways to justify what I did but there was no excuse.

"I have to tell her now, that's it." I told Abraham once Vanessa had darted away into the kitchen to get herself a drink.

"NO, you don't. If you want to live, you will strategically plan how you're going to break the news to her. She doesn't deserve this news to be thrown at her so thoughtlessly." He muttered back.

"You're right. What about telling her over a candlelight dinner?"

"Candlelight dinner? You really don't get it." He shook his head

"You're right. That's a fire hazard. That can end bad"

I knew what Abraham was implying. It took me a minute to man up and accept it. "I have to make her fall out of love with me, don't I?"

"Yes. And in love with someone else,"

Those words felt like a bullet in my chest. "I'd rather go blind before I watch her fall in love with someone else," I told him.

"It's not a bad idea. Think about it. She finds someone else to love and it will be easier for her to accept your truth."

It didn't sound like a bad idea, or maybe we were just

two ignorant men thinking we had this shit under control when clearly we didn't. "Vanessa won't be able to fall in love with another man," I told him.

"Vanessa is human. If you neglect her long enough, eventually she will entertain being with someone else. And that's what we want. It's the only way, man."

"It's going to be hard. She's going to fight for us."

"And you're going to let her fight alone."

I hated the man I was becoming. No matter how bad the news, Vanessa would want me to tell her the truth and not sugar coat anything, but I just couldn't do it. Just then, Vanessa came back, her excitement level still high.

"Oh, you guys... I forgot. One more surprise."

I rushed over to her, feeling taunted by anything else she would have to say. "Baby, how about you save it for later."

Abraham agreed. "Yeah, girl. You can't spoil us with all this good news at once."

She wouldn't take no for an answer. She continued, "Since I'm an obstetrician, we decided it'd be great if I delivered the baby." She pinched my cheeks. "Oh, don't be jealous. We'll have our baby this year too. Then they'll all grow up together. Right, Abraham? Zoe's baby, our baby, and your's and Jordy's baby!"

"Yup, good plan, Vanessa." Grabbing his coat, he said,

"Listen, I have to leave. Jordy wants ice cream. You know cravings and shit. But Chase, I want you to meet someone tomorrow. Ruth's Chris, eight o'clock."

"Yeah, I'll be there," I said.

Vanessa cleared her throat. "Correction. *We* will be there," she said.

"Just a guy's night out," Abraham yelled from the door.

"Okay, but after tomorrow he's all mine and we're going to start working on making that baby," she said, running her hands up my back. She kissed me softly and walked away. My emotions were spinning around me. There was no way I'd let Vanessa throw her life away for me. All of this baggage I was now bringing along on this journey was unacceptable.

As soon as Vanessa went to bed, I took a drive to our beach house on Long Island, where Zoe was staying. My blood was boiling as I approached Zoe, who was sitting on the front porch at one in the morning, manically smoking a cigarette. Surprised to see me, she took one last puff and threw the cigarette to the ground before rushing to get in the house. I grabbed her by the arm and tried to yank her out until I saw a neighbor sitting on the porch. I decided to follow Zoe inside.

"You conniving, malicious little bitch!" I shouted at her.

"Chase, I swear, it wasn't supposed to go that far. You never liked me and that night I saw you at the bar, it was my chance to change that. I just wanted you to get to know me for me."

I admit I never gave Zoe a chance. Out of all the years she'd been around, I never had any interest in getting to know her. The one time I met her, I saw right through her. Who "stops in" to their best friend's wedding then darts out before staying even an hour? There was always something off about her, like her soul gave off bad vibes. No matter how much time Nessa invested in fixing her, she was damaged and broken beyond repair and I had always wished that Nessa would cut her loose.

"Well, now I know you really *good*," I sneered. "I know you're positive."

Zoe was speechless at my words, but from her facial expression I could tell she'd known about her diagnosis for some time now. "There's no way you could have gotten the virus. My viral load is undetectable, Chase. A positive person with an undetectable viral load is less likely to transmit the disease--"

"Are you trying to educate me about HIV? I'm the doctor and you're nothing but the ghetto hood-rat I always told Nessa you were."

For the first time I looked in her eyes, realizing how true it was that people who hurt will always try to hurt others. She stared at me, chewing her thumbnail. "And you're nothing but the dog that I always told Nessa you were. Now get out!"

This only boiled my blood more. "How dare you gamble with her life? Gamble with mine? After everything she's done for you. You did this on purpose, didn't you? You always wanted everything she had and the moment you found out we were planning to start a family, you fucked that up too." I was so angry, I felt like I could kill her. "Undetectable, detectable. Guess what? You're still positive." As the words exited from my mouth, my own reality set in and I fell to my knees in tears. "You gave me a virus I can't cure. I can't sleep with my wife now."

She rushed to the floor, trying to embrace me. "But you can sleep with her, Chase. You can love her the same. If you take the antiretroviral therapy it will control it and...."

I pushed her off, sending her flying into the wall. "What kind of person are you? You knowingly fucked your best friend's husband and now you want me to risk her life?"

With no emotion at all, she continued, "And you willingly cheated. It's not like I put a gun to your head." She stood up with the intention to walk away but stopped in her tracks when she heard my gun cock. I brought it along with me with no intention to use it, but I didn't trust Zoe, and realized a confrontation with her could be dangerous.

"What if I put one in your head instead?"

She carefully raised her hands into the air and as she did, I envisioned her blood splattered all over the walls and her body slumped over, lifeless. A sense of evil washed over me, making me feel like pulling that trigger would be the perfect compensation for the chaos this bitch had brought to my life. I was disgusted by this shell of a woman and was convinced I should play God.

"Chase, please put the gun down." Zoe turned around slowly, fear written all over her face. "If you kill me, you kill our baby, and no matter how fucked up the situation is, this baby is innocent. So please, just put the gun down."

I had forgotten all about the baby, if there really was one. I grabbed her by the neck looking into her eyes. "I should kill you right here, right now. I should kill you and walk away." The only thing that stopped me was the sonogram picture she quickly pulled out of her pocket. I let her loose and she gasped for air. "You make me sick. You are evil." I crumbled the sonogram picture up and threw it at her. "If you don't regret this now, one day you will." I walked out praying I had the strength to not return.

Sleeping in my car that night made Nessa assume I was out doing something I wasn't supposed to be doing. This was just the start of making her fall out of love with me. I ignored her calls and didn't go home to freshen up or change. Instead, I sat at a bar all day until it was time to meet Abraham at the restaurant he suggested we go. When I spotted Vanessa there, waiting for me like an angry black woman, I texted Abraham a new location. She didn't see me. I lingered a while just to admire her from afar. She was so beautiful, even when she got mad.

Approaching the new restaurant, I found Abraham already seated with a friend I had never met before. They had already gotten started on food and drinks.

Abraham gave me a look. "I'm not even going to ask."

I sat down and sipped his water. "Please don't," I said.

He continued twirling spaghetti around his fork and then shoving it directly in his mouth. "This is Lance, the FBI director who works with me," he explained with his mouth full. "I told him a little bit about our situation."

Thank God the waitress came over at just that moment to interrupt the awkward introduction. "I see we have another guest," she said. "Can I get you something?"

"I'll take what he's having," I said, pointing to Abraham's meal.

After she walked away, I extended my hand to the friend. "I'm Chase."

Not knowing where to begin, I let Abraham take the lead. "I was thinking he would be the perfect match for Nessa," he told me.

"Well, I didn't agree to anything just yet," Lance said.

Then Abraham joked, "But you owe me a favor so it really isn't up to you."

"This is more than just a favor and definitely doesn't

compare to you playing Santa for me last year," Lance said.

Every year the guys at their field office picked one person to dress up as Santa and give out gifts at the mall for a charity called "Tis the Season to Give."

"I don't understand, though" he said, "this is your wife you're setting up?"

"I wouldn't call it setting up, but yes. It's my wife, who I love very much. I need to make her fall out of love with me. That's my job. Yours is simple. Make her fall in love with you."

"When are you trying to make this happen?" he asked.

Abraham answered, "The sooner the better. ASAP."

I was annoyed with Abraham for moving so fast without my permission, but he and I both know that I would have procrastinated.

"Slow down, I need a little more time, please," this was all moving so fast. "I think you should officially meet her on her birthday," I suggested.

"When is that?"

"December 18. She already has two tickets to poetry night at that club on Dyker Street."

"December 18. Aren't you already committed to being Santa that night?" Abraham asked.

"Yeah but I should be able to make it to the club later that night. Unless you want to take over this year?" he asked

Abraham, who promptly got up from the table.

"No more favors," Abraham joked. "I'll be back."

After Abraham left us alone, I took a closer look at this man. Maybe he was a little too perfect? We talked for a while, and in that time he told me he had it all, but he was missing one thing in his life: a woman on his level. Nessa was definitely that.

"Now tell me about her," he insisted.

Without hesitation, I did just that. I told him how from the minute I first gazed upon her, I knew I had to have her. That she would be mine forever. I wanted her in the most innocent sense. She was average at five-foot four, but not at all average. There was something that separated her from other females. Initially I was attracted to her physique as any man would have been.

I first saw her when we were both in medical school. It was my last year and her first year. It was warm and bright that day, and even the sun seemed intrigued by her smooth caramel skin. She was heaven sent. Her rose-petal lips cracked a smile and her laugh set the hairs on my neck to stand on end. I didn't believe in love at first sight until my eyes witnessed such perfection.

I contemplated whether it would be a good idea to approach her. The last thing we as med students needed was distraction. But on the other hand, sometimes the one thing we needed as med students was distraction.

Catching me off guard, she spoke to me first. "You know it's not polite to stare." Her voice was so warm and comforting.

"I'm sorry I honestly didn't realize I was being so rude," I told her. "I hope I didn't offend you."

"No, not offended," she said, shaking her head with a slight smirk.

"I was a bit lost in my thoughts," I admitted.

"Well, now I'm curious to know what you were thinking."

For the second time in our conversation, I was caught in the headlights. She was the first woman who'd ever been able to render me speechless and I became even more intrigued.

"So, you're kind of doing that whole staring thing again," she joked. "Have we met before?"

"No, I don't believe we have. I'm just not sure how to tell you how beautiful you are without sounding completely creepy." I managed to force a smile hoping she would too.

"Well, honestly, the blank stares aren't exactly the most convincing strategy," she teased. "I'm Vanessa. My friends call me Nessa." Her inviting brown eyes washed away my insecurities.

I was no longer intimidated, and more so determined to make her a friend, at the least. "I'm Chase, and my friends call me Chase."

Her beautiful smile took over her entire face.

"That's what I want to do," I said. She looked at me like I was nuts. "I want to make you smile like that. A smile is produced by two types of muscles. The orbicularis oculi muscles reveal the true feelings of a genuine smile--"

"While the zygomatic face muscle is controlled. In other words, used to produce false smiles."

I wasn't expecting that, but her intellectual capacity made me more eager. "So I assume you also have the dreadful pleasure of taking AFA 113."

"And I assume you're prepared for next week's exam. But I never had anyone use the anatomy of face muscles as a pickup line before."

"Well I guess I'm that devoted to my studies."

She giggled softly then replied, "So devoted that you'd incorporate it into your social life?"

"I'd love to incorporate you into my social life," I said, without missing a beat.

"The way you were looking at me, you'd probably love to incorporate me into your bed," she joked.

"Yes, I want to sleep with you. Am I wrong for

wanting that?"

Her glow of happiness immediately turned into displeasure and disgust as she rolled her eyes and muttered, "A waste of my damn time," before turning to walk away from me.

"Nessa!" I called after her but she ignored me and continued walking into the school building. "Nessa!"

Just when I was about to chase her inside, she turned back around, charging at me like a bull. "Do not call me Nessa. Only my friends are allowed to call me Nessa and you are not my friend!" She poked my chest forcefully with her index finger. "My name is Vanessa to you, mister."

"You don't understand," I told her. "I want to sleep with you in the most innocent sense of the phrase. I want to hold you all night while I fall asleep to your voice and the smell of your scent. I want to cuddle with you. I want to know your fears, your dreams. I want to know what your childhood was like. I want to know if you snore because I swear I would tease you for the rest of our lives together. I want to wake up staring into your brown eyes. I don't want your naked body without working for it. Your naked body should only belong to those who fall in love with your naked soul."

There was a moment of silence as we faced each other, trying to figure out each other's next thoughts. "Please, Nessa." I stuttered a little. "Is it okay if I call you Nessa?"

"Did you learn that from school too?" she asked, *sarcasm in her tone.*

"No, that came from the heart."

She stared at me for about five seconds before speaking again. "Sorry I left fingerprints on your heart."

Abraham had returned, and he and Lance had their eyes fixed on me as I finished my story.

"Nessa must be a very special lady," said Lance. "You place her on a pedestal it seems not even heaven can reach. I would love to meet her."

CHAPTER 10

Vanessa, May 2013

Present Day

Zoe became motionless as a large amount of water trickled from between her legs. She started crying hysterically, "I'm only thirty-seven weeks. This is too early."

I assured her, "You can go in two weeks before your due date or after. This is completely normal."

I didn't press her further about how she knew about the supermarket. I hadn't come to terms with it yet, or been able to process it. There is no way she would have known about the grocery run if she hadn't been on the phone with Chase earlier.

Why would Chase have been on the phone with Zoe? I brushed it off, but I didn't forget it.

Day by day my guard had been going up as she started to lose my trust. Trust was a fragile thing. Easy to break, easy to lose, and one of the hardest things to get back. Zoe was on the verge of losing mine for good.

But now was not the time to discuss it. Her labor pains started kicking in and her contractions quickly went from ten minutes apart to two. They came fast and strong. I began doing Lamaze with her, something I had taught her during her pregnancy. The focused breathing was supposed to help her relax through labor, but it was having the complete opposite effect and she panicked more.

I was committed to her pregnancy like I was the father. Zoe didn't have a companion to comfort her but through the ups and downs she could always count on me. Zoe had explained when she first told me about the pregnancy that the baby's father didn't want anything to do with them. Another fatherless child coming into this world broke my heart. I couldn't tell you how many fathers were absent for the birth of their child. How many birth certificates were missing signatures. I had seen it all. This child's soul will form a hole no man could fill besides a dad.

Knowing Zoe, the father was probably some random married man with his own family. After all, Zoe loved fucking married men. That didn't justify his absence, but I could understand it. If Chase ever stepped out on me and impregnated another woman, I'd definitely encourage him to be in that child's life, no matter what happened between us.

When we were leaving for the hospital, Chase offered to drive us even though we hadn't been on the best of terms for months. I sat in the back seat with Zoe, comforting her through the pain. I watched Chase drive like a mad man, sweat glistening on his face. It was actually cute seeing how nervous he was. Then jealousy took over as I only imagined it being the other way around. Chase driving as Zoe sat in the back seat with me in labor. But it wasn't the time to be selfish, and I pushed the thought away.

Although I had been falling hard for Lance, my heart stayed open to making things work with the man I took my vows with. I thought maybe he was coming around, and this was the start of fixing things. When we arrived at the hospital, he came in with us. He didn't take off like I thought he might. I was overjoyed he'd put his differences with Zoe aside. I couldn't help but wonder if he was really even talking to her over the phone. I had to prep for the delivery and I wanted someone to be with her.

"The parents-to-be can come with me," said the nurse.

A little blindsided, I corrected her. "Oh, no, he isn't the dad. We're family. Here to support."

"I'm so sorry. In that case, the mom-to-be can come with me, and Dr. Moretti, you can go and get ready. We will have her regular physician send over all prenatal screening and test results."

"Thank you so much," I said, then turned to Chase. "And thank you for being here. You didn't have to do this."

"Please don't mention it," he said.. "I wanted to be here. I had to be here."

Zoe shouted in pain as they took her down the hall.

"If I could take her pain away I would, but I can't. Can you stay with her until I finish prepping?" I asked him.

"Yeah, sure. Anything for you." He moved to kiss me on my forehead once again, but I grabbed his face and kissed his lips for the first time in a very long time. It didn't feel the same.

Zoe's test results were sent in. I expected everything to come back normal but that was when I learned my best friend was HIV-positive, and she had never told me. It should have been a time of happiness, but I couldn't help but cry. She asked me to deliver her baby because she trusted I would bring the baby into the world HIV-negative, and that was my plan.

When I got to the delivery room to discuss the options she had for delivery, there was Chase, holding her hands through the pain. I appreciated what he was doing but it also unnerved me. I've delivered plenty of babies, and to me, he looked like the nervous expectant dad, and was acting like it too.

"I'm going to go get more ice chips for her," he said when I arrived, and he headed out.

Zoe reached out to wipe my face. "We can't both be in here crying," she said.

I flipped into business mode. "Well, I have good news for you. The level of virus circulating in your blood is undetectable. This means you can have a vaginal delivery."

"Are you sure? Is it safe?"

"Yes, it's safe. It would have been safer if you had told me sooner rather than later. You know I would have protected you."

She gave a weak smile. "Yes, I know, Nessa. Like you've protected me all these years. Thank you, for everything."

"What happened to the promise we made to never keep secrets from each other?" I lightly kissed her on her forehead and reassured her. "No matter what, you are my sister. Always and forever."

Even a blind person could see she was hurting and that her pain ran deeper than labor pains. The way she looked at me made me feel as if there was so much more she wanted to say but in that moment, I cut her off. "Not now. We have a lifetime to catch up. Let's just bring my godchild into this world, happy and healthy."

Then, in the blink of an eye, the entire staff rushed the room. The baby's heart rate had dropped and we had to move fast.

Zoe asked horrified, "Nessa, what's happening?"

We raced her to the OR and as we passed Chase, he dropped the cup of ice chips he was holding. At that moment, all the pieces came together, but I forced myself to put them away. I fully understood why he was here, but I couldn't think about it now. In a robotic tone, I explained to Zoe, "We have to perform an emergency C-section. It has nothing to do with you. The baby's heart rate has dropped." My emotions went numb, as if I had been injected with the anesthesia given to Zoe to numb her lower body before surgery.

My hands started shaking as I made a horizontal incision. She had had a C-section before. Another thing that had come up in her medical records that she never told me about. She had given birth to a baby girl at the tender age of sixteen. Now it all made sense. She moved to Los Angeles, and I never knew about any of it. Zoe was full of secrets, and today was the day everything was coming to light. Placing my hand underneath the head, I pulled the baby out. Keeping the baby safe was my only concern.

It was a boy! A beautiful, healthy boy. I held my husband's baby in my arms for a few seconds before he was taken away for tests.

Stitching the patient up was always like putting a puzzle together – one that I usually enjoyed. Today I didn't enjoy any of it. There were so many pieces of this puzzle missing. Without those pieces, I would never understand why the two people I loved the most had betrayed me like this.

"When the anesthesia wears off and you can feel your body come back to life, I will bring the baby to you."

Zoe reached out to me. "Thank you so much," she said, but I walked away from her.

"Nessa! What's wrong?" she called after me.

I charged back at her. "*You're* what's wrong. You're lucky I don't beat your ass in this hospital bed, you trifling bitch."

The nurses looked up with concern but continued with their work.

Tears poured down her face. "Nessa, I'm so sorry. It was a mistake. It wasn't Chase's fault. Please." She tried getting up to run after me but ended up falling to the floor as her body was still pretty much paralyzed. The nurses rushed over to help. As for me, I was done rescuing her. She could have died on that floor and it would have made no difference to me.

My husband, the man I had stood at the altar with, was standing by the nursery, watching his baby sleep.

I stood by his side for the last time. "He looks just like you." Chase remained mute, so I continued, "He will be tested at one month, three months, and six months. If all three tests are negative, which I strongly believe they will be, he will be considered HIV negative."

With tears in his eyes, he said, "I'm so sorry, Nessa."

"Everyone is so sorry. Sorry, sorry, sorry. Sorry won't change a goddamned thing. You broke me. You watched me break into a million pieces and you left me there, thinking I had done something wrong when all along it was you."

"Do you think it was easy for me to do that? I couldn't touch you. I couldn't make love to you. I had to stop loving you. That's how much I love you."

"You stopped loving me, and that was the best thing you could have ever done."

Stuttering from the guilt, he tried explaining how everything happened. "I had a bad surgery that day. I was supposed to save that little girl but she died. She died on my operating table. You were gone for almost two months and--"

Interrupting him, I snapped back. "So it's my fault?"

"No! It's my fault, Nessa, for not respecting our marriage, for stepping out on you, for not telling you sooner. But please believe me, I had no idea it was Zoe. She introduced herself as Destiny." He grabbed my arm, "Why the fuck would she do that?"

"Whether I believe you or not, it doesn't change the fact that you threw our lives away for a piece of pussy." I wanted to snap my fingers and be in the privacy of my home so that I could really give him a piece of my mind but I was at work and I had to keep it professional. "Maybe you should just go ahead and see how she's doing." Feeling a tad bit curious I asked him, "Have you thought of a name?"

Scathingly, he replied, "Lance is a good name, isn't it?"

I couldn't believe he knew about Lance. Was Zoe so conniving that she went behind my back and told him about my affair too? I fumbled with words that felt like a stone in my throat. "Lance is a good name. Lance is actually a good man. A good fuck too, but definitely a good man."

I wanted to hurt him just as bad as he hurt me but it was like he was on a mission, "I know he's a good man. You deserve a good man, Nessa. I can't give you your happily ever after. Maybe he can."

"NO!" I screamed at him. "You don't get to call me Nessa. Only my friends are allowed to call me that. You and that bitch are dead to me."

The knots in my stomach convinced me it was time to go. There was nothing left for me to say.

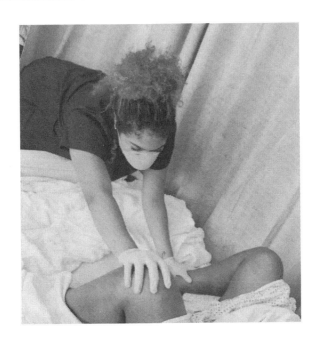

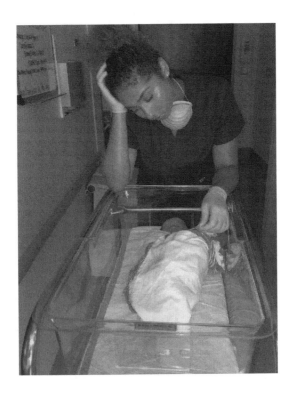

CHAPTER 11

Vanessa, May 2013

I had loved Chase despite his flaws and insecurities. I never judged him. I never wanted perfect -- perfect doesn't exist. I asked for a human to love and to love me in return. I gave Chase a love that could quiet any storm, but I guess it wasn't strong enough to end a war.

I couldn't stop thinking about it. How they fucked. Where they fucked. When they fucked. I cried out in agony, then yelled at myself to shut up. My mind became a ticking time bomb as I tried to piece it all together. I felt I would explode if I didn't find peace within the truth. When the smoke finally cleared, who knew who would survive.

Choking on my tears, I started to hyperventilate. I called the one person I needed the most at a time like this. "Hello, Mom," I slurred.

No matter how many miles away, a mother's love can cure the deepest cut. "What's wrong, baby?" Hearing her voice brought me peace and a few seconds of happiness. It was always something about that question being asked that always made me break down even more. I couldn't summon up the strength to explain anything.

She listened to my cries and said what I needed to hear: "Come home baby."

I was too vulnerable to speak.

"Hello, did you hear what I said? Come home, Vanessa, now!"

So much was racing through my mind, it took me a moment to collect myself to be able to respond. "Okay."

Thinking about my failed marriage made my head throb. I walked into the kitchen and ransacked the bar for a bottle of Hennessy. "I've given you the best years of my life and this is what you do? I invested my time, my body, my soul, and you betray me like this. You play me like this?" The burn of cognac against my tongue and throat was my only cure for now. "The love of your life. Haaaa! There's no such thing as the love of your life. You love someone today and you hate them tomorrow," I said while sloppily gliding down the hall, shuffling my drunken feet. I noticed pictures of us on the walls – they reminded me of how happy we were at one point. Now they fueled my despair. "What did I do to deserve this?"

Ripping those memories off of the wall brought a feeling of relief and pleasure, so I continued fucking shit up. Chase had given me the best memories, and sadly, he would end up being just that. A memory. I looked at our wedding picture for a moment before smashing it to bits. "Another memory you will fucking become. A memory that fades away every day. And with each day that passes, each and every single scar you left on my heart will fade away too."

I stood in front of the bathroom mirror. "They say give the man rope to hang himself. I give a little bit of rope and you hang the fucking both of us?" Clenching my fist, I forcefully punched my reflection. I was now a broken girl living in a shattered world, and each piece that had fallen to the floor was a dissection of me.

My fist was brutally swollen and throbbing with pain, but that didn't stop me. Everything in my home that reminded me of Chase was shredded like a piece of scrap paper. "He made a mistake. No! He *was* the mistake! Coming into my life and fucking shit up. Why was this happening to me, God? Why, why, why, me? This can't be!"

And Zoe... She was my best friend! She was my sister! "And that trifling bitch. Holding a knife behind my back -- but that's okay. That same knife she stabbed me with I'm taking away and cutting myself lose from the both of them." I felt like Bernie Burns from *Waiting to Exhale*. What's that saying? "Hell hath no fury like a woman scorned." Right.

Hours had passed, and I was sitting in a house filled with bad vibes and chaos. My suitcases were waiting for me at the door. Some might argue that his suitcases should have been packed and I should have put him out, but the truth is there is no force more powerful than a woman walking away from a life that wronged her and that can no longer serve her. We have to leave the good, the bad, and the ugly where they're at in order to move on and create something better. I left everything I knew, along with my wedding dress, burning to dust, and I finally signed those divorce papers. I was ready to drive off to my parents' house and never look back.

Before starting the car, I gently laid my head on the steering wheel and sobbed. Feeling sick, I took a few deep breaths before starting the car and pulling out of the driveway. There was nothing I could do to get peace of mind. While trying to gain composure, I patted myself down for my phone. My heartbeat accelerated as I scrolled through all of my missed calls and messages. Chase had been calling nonstop. I turned my phone off.

When I looked into the rearview mirror I saw a monster. The tears couldn't stop falling, and as I tried to wipe them away, my mascara smeared down my caramel cheeks. I wiped so hard my false eyelash fell off and into my lap.

It was a very hot Tuesday in New York, and the traffic into Baltimore was bumper to bumper. The drive took almost five hours, but I finally made it. My mom and stepdad greeted me on the porch with bright smiles and cheerful waves. My biological father passed away when I was three and Ronnie had come into my life when I was six. He'd treated me like I was his daughter ever since.

I paused a moment before exiting my vehicle. Ronnie approached, giving me a kiss on the forehead. Perfect for a stepdad. Alarming when Chase had kissed me that way, I felt far from secure.

"Hi baby girl!"

"Hi Daddy," I said, not looking at him because I didn't want him to see my swollen eyes.

He wasn't fooled. He lifted my chin. "Keep your head up or your crown will slip, my queen."

He winked and I smiled back at him as he grabbed my bags. I was definitely a daddy's girl. Before we got to the house, he bluntly said, "I'll have to take a look at that hand, too."

There was nothing I could hide from him. He knew me so well. I remember when I was a kid and he took me to Bring Your Kids to Work Day. That was the day I decided I wanted to be a doctor.

My mother ran to me, wrapping her arms around me holding me tight. "I'm so happy you're home, baby. I hope you're hungry because I made Sunday dinner on a Tuesday."

"Ah, I'm starving, Ma!"

There is nothing like being around family. We ate, talked, laughed, and cried together. Being back home reminded me of my childhood. The good ol' days when life was simple. Zoe and I actually had some good memories in this house. Every weekend we used to stay up girl-chatting about boys and our future, sneaking out of my bedroom window on a Saturday night to sit on top of the roof. which made us feel like we were sitting on top of the world. Sunday mornings would find us asleep in church.

We had been glued at the hip like Bonnie and Clyde. Zoe had had a rough childhood, but because I loved her so much, my parents helped give her a better life. They had also diagnosed me with "only child syndrome," and believed this was a good way to break free from that.

Zoe was fifteen when she moved in with us because Momma Tone, the woman who had taken care of her, was sick. My family and I ended up moving to Baltimore that same year, leaving Zoe behind. She had made the decision to stay in New York until Momma Tone had gotten out of the hospital, but some things never go as planned. Momma Tone ended up passing away that same year, forcing Zoe to move back in with her biological mom and step-dad. I had begged Zoe to move to Baltimore, that was the original plan, but she refused. Shortly after, Zoe had moved far away to the West Coast but I never really knew why. I guess being secretly pregnant and giving birth might have been the reason she left New York behind, wanting a fresh start.

No matter what Zoe did, I still thought of her as my sister. Especially in the presence of my parents. My heart couldn't stop loving her but now it would definitely be love from a distance.

There wasn't anything better than the comfort of my parent's home, curled up underneath my favorite blanket, eating butter pecan ice cream.

I contemplated turning my phone back on. I wanted to speak to Lance before going to sleep, but a million messages and voicemails rushed in from Chase. I decided to read his sorry-ass apologies but when I opened one of the messages, my heart came to a halt. The doorbell rang at the same time, but I couldn't move to open it. It was Chase. My mother and I screamed out in agony at the same time.

It was Zoe. She had suffered an amniotic fluid embolism that caused her to go into cardiac arrest. Zoe was dead.

CHAPTER 12

Vanessa, May 2013

The clouds embraced in the sky, changing its color from a soft blue to a dark grey and hiding the sun. Raindrops fell onto the majestic white and gold casket as it lowered into the ground.

The atmosphere definitely matched my emotions. It was gloomy and lifeless outside, and inside I felt empty and weak. I stumbled into Lance's arms as he offered me his shoulder to lean on. The pink and white roses that covered Zoe's casket reminded me of her beauty. But they, too, would soon die. We were supposed to grow grey and old together, sharing memories with our children and our grandchildren. The lower the casket dropped, the more I lost control.

Looking around, I saw Chase and the baby, who was dressed in white, symbolizing purity. I was surprised to see Zoe's parents attend the burial. I never really knew them. Zoe's mother was a drug addict, and also blind. The only person I knew that Zoe considered a mother was Momma Tone, but she passed when Zoe was sixteen years old. They had another child with them who was in her teens and who looked identical to Zoe. I couldn't help but wonder if this was the child that came up in Zoe's medical records.

The crowd began to dissipate, and soon I was the only one standing at the grave. When Zoe's family approached me, out of respect I told them, "I'm so sorry for your loss. I hope you all can find a way to get through this."

"It's not a loss, it's a blessing."

I was shocked at the girl's response. I didn't say anything though, as I understood her anger.

Zoe's mother finally broke her silence. "Is it true? Is she dead?" She snatched her sunglasses off of her face, revealing her blindness, "I don't remember what she looks like. I only remember the scent of her. I remember the touch of her. She was only nine years old when she briefly moved back in with me because her father had died. She ran away the next day and came back six years later."

"Ms. Fallon, when Zoe came back home, she was fifteen years old. How long did she stay with you the second time?" I questioned her.

"She stayed for about ten months a year the most." She sobbed.

I spoke to the beautiful girl, now looking impatient to leave. I knew exactly who she was now. "I feel like I've seen you before," I told her.

"No, I don't think we've met. Grandma, let's go home. I don't know why we came here in the first place."

Confirming what I already knew, Zoe's mother continued, "Zelle, she was my daughter and she was your mother. You should be able to say a proper goodbye."

"Why is it necessary to say goodbye when I never even got the chance to say hello? I never met her when she was alive. Why should this be the only memory I have of her?"

I stood there speechless and confused. I was sure this was the young girl Zoe and I had seen in the mall on my birthday. I wanted to tell them how great Zoe was and how much they had missed out, but it seems it was the other way around.

Zelle walked off and into the arms of a man who looked like he could have been her father, but he was so old he looked like he could also be her *step*-grandfather. "Ms. Fallon," I asked, treading carefully. "Is that Zelle's dad?"

She laughed. "It's funny, you know. Everyone always tells me Zelle looks like that man. But that's not the funny part. Do you want to know the funny part?"

I nodded my head at first until I remembered she couldn't see, "I can definitely use a laugh right about now."

"That man is Zoe's stepfather."

For clarity, I asked, "So that means he would have no real connection to Zelle. So how do they look so much alike?"

She resumed crying, and I just hugged her tightly. "I came to say sorry to my baby," She wept. "I hope she hears me. I hope she forgives me."

It was at this moment that I understood that logic was behind every choice Zoe had ever made. When I realized what had happened to her, I could not imagine what she went through with that man. That inner turmoil she held on to changed her life for sure.

"Do you think he's doing the same thing to Zelle?" she asked me.

I looked in their direction, and although I wanted to say yes, I instead said, "I can't say for sure, Ms. Fallon, but I can help y'all start over. Let me help you."

We took slow steps to the car reminiscing about Zoe. She thanked me for the role I played in her daughter's life. Approaching the car, I begged her, "Please think about it."

I walked to my car to find Chase sitting in the passenger seat. "I don't have the strength to fight you."

"Then don't."

"I can't take any more bad news, Chase, and there's nothing good coming from you, so why are you here?"

"I named him Calum, which means 'peace'."

I forgot what peace felt like. I would die right now for a piece of peace. "That's a beautiful name. Are you happy?"

"How can I be happy? I lost the love of my life and she lost her best friend."

I started my car up. "Listen, I have to go."

"Before Zoe passed away, she mentioned something about a book she was writing."

"More secrets. She never told me anything about a book."

"She said you would know where to find it. That you have the key."

Nonchalantly, I said, "I'll look into it," but deep down I was anxious to find the book. I knew exactly where it was. We both had these pink safety boxes that held memories inside. She had a key to mine and I had one to hers. *This can mean closure for everyone.* I reached over him to open the passenger door. "I really have to go, Chase."

"I can't do this on my own, Vanessa. I need your help."

I was a bit confused. "You need my help with what?"

"I don't want Calum to grow up without a mother."

"So, you're asking me to be his mother? I'm flattered."

"Please, Vanessa."

I yelled at the top of my lungs, every single bitter emotion I felt inside propelling the words out of me: "I am not his mother! Get out!"

"Vanessa, please just think about it," he said before getting out of my car.

The only thing I can think about was life without Zoe. I

reminisced a little and cried some more. It hurt so bad that Zoe wasn't here to wipe my tears away.

CHAPTER 13

Vanessa: 2017

Four Years Later

For the past four years, I have woken up every morning telling myself, *I am going to fight this, I am going to survive.* And I have done just that. I have survived the war. It took me some time but I made it.

The process of healing and finding peace was my main priority. I do not believe that time heals all wounds. In time, the pain lessens but the memories and the scars remain. Wounds left in my heart have slowly but surely faded into battle scars.

I feel now, as I felt then, that God gives his toughest battles to his strongest soldiers. It is the pain that we encounter throughout our lives that will most definitely break us before it helps shape us and make us who we are. Finding beauty within your scars is the truest thing for the soul because, darling, the most beautiful parts of us have bruises, scratches, cracks, and dents too.

Nothing in this life is perfect, not even the American dream. That white picket fence doesn't always come along with a man and a ring, or kids and puppies. Sometimes it's just you, on your own, and that is okay too. I had a million reasons to cry, but I had one good reason to smile. My family. My white picket fence came along with a package.

"Momma, get up. We have to go to Zelle's graduation. We're going to be late."

I was exhausted from setting up for the party all night, and I felt like I had just fallen asleep. I got up in a panic thinking I was late but when I looked at the clock, it was only 5:45. "Calum, baby, it's too early to go to Zelle's graduation."

"But Mommy, I'm ready to go." Calum was dressed and ready from head to toe. He and our poodle, Brownie, pulled the covers off of me, while trying to pull me out of bed. Calum was definitely the perfect little blessing that I found peace in. "Pops cooked breakfast, Momma."

I picked him up, "How about you and Pops go get started without me?"

"So, you can get ready and then we can go?"

Playfully I asked him, "How'd you know that?"

"Because I'm the smartest little boy in the world that you love very much."

I put him down. "How much do I love you?"

He opened his arms as wide as he could spread them, "You love me this much," he said, and ran off.

I tried to sit up and put my legs over the side of the bed.

At this point in my pregnancy, I couldn't even see my feet. My stomach felt like it had grown bigger overnight.

Just then, Calum ran back to me. "Oh, Mommy! I forgot to give my baby sister a morning kiss." He kissed my stomach then ran downstairs.

Calum was excited to be a big brother and I was happy to give him that title. From the day he was born I'd fallen in love with him. There was no way I could have turned my back on him. I got dressed and headed down for breakfast.

"Oh look, there's our queen, Calum."

I couldn't help but blush. "And there's my king and my little prince."

"And our princess is baking in the oven, right Momma?" Calum shouted from the table.

After being broken, you are obligated to pick up those pieces and put yourself back together. Love everything about you because there will be someone waiting to love all up on your flaws and imperfections, so whatever you do, embrace those battle scars and insecurities.

I kissed Lance on the lips and Calum covered his eyes. "Calum, are you excited to see Daddy today?"

"Yes!" he screamed out in excitement. "I can't wait to tell him all about my new game."

"Good, because he's excited to see you, too."

Calum understood that his dad and I loved each other very much, but just because two people love each other doesn't mean they belong together. I believe Chase's purpose in my life was to help me become a better woman for Lance. Out of respect and love, Calum called Lance "Pops" and Chase "Daddy." Chase had a good attitude about it, and always told Calum, "You're a lucky little guy to have two dads."

Before leaving the house, Calum picked up a picture of Zoe and me he always gravitated to. "Mommy, when are you going to tell me about this lady you're with?"

"That's my best friend, Zoe."

Before I could finish, Calum impersonated me and the words he had heard me say so many times before. "One day I'll tell you all about her, but today there isn't enough time."

I laughed it off and kneeled down, kissing Calum on his forehead. "Calum, just trust me."

That was my truth. One day I would tell him all about the woman who gave birth to him. For now, he was too young to understand and as his mother, I had to protect him.

Lance left for work while Calum and I left to meet Chase and attend Zelle's college graduation. I was so proud of her. She reminded me of her mother at this age. Zelle was graduating top of her class from Princeton University. After Zoe's funeral, Zelle and I built a friendship no one can break. Thankfully Zelle had never been sexually abused by Zoe's stepfather, who was really Zelle's father, and had pretended all these years to be Zelle's grandfather.

He begged me not to tell her the truth about her mother until she finished college. I explained to him that it wasn't my place to say anything, but that one day she would know the truth. Chase and I gifted Zelle with her college education, but today I would give her another gift: her mother's memoir. She was now an adult, and in order to move forward in this world she would need to know her family's truth. Hopefully one day Zelle would forgive her mother as I have done.

Once I read Zoe's book, everything became clear. I understood her more deeply, and one day all of you will too. She never got the chance to write the perfect ending, so I wrote one for her. One that she would be proud of. *Naked Soul: The Zoelyn Story.*

Everyone seems to be in good spirits at this point in our lives, especially me. I never thought I'd make it back to a happy place in my life but I did. After divorcing Chase, I learned to love myself again. I made a promise to myself that I'd never get married again. Sometimes promises are meant to be broken because here I am engaged and planning a wedding. I can't say for sure if this is my happily ever after, I'm not sure if I believe in those anymore. But I will say this: I am alive, blessed, and happiness does exist.

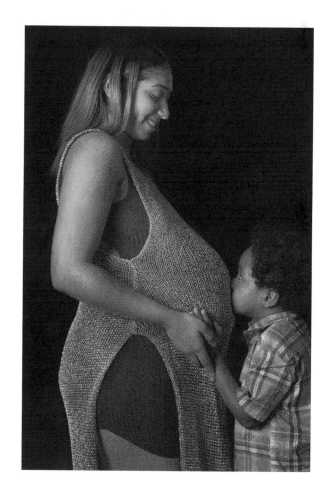

Author's Note

I wrote *Naked Soul* to bring a powerful yet relatable story to life. The challenges my characters face are issues real people grapple with in their actual lives. Many homes and hearts have been broken by infidelity. Even if you're not able to directly relate to marital infidelity or the consequences, it's likely you've been betrayed by a loved one on some level in your life.

There is no such thing as a perfect being, and we see that as Chase's character develops. Chase shows us that we are always one decision away from a life filled with regret. For Chase, one bad decision causes him to lose everything, except his love for Vanessa. "I love you so much that I had to stop loving you" is one of my favorite quotes from *Naked Soul*. At times, our judgement can get clouded, and when our emotions and sense of logic are not well aligned, it's best we remain still and let God take over.

I put a lot of thought into Vanessa's character and I had a lot of fun developing her. Vanessa is me. She is you. She is every female. She is a warrior. The conflicts she encounters break her temporarily but they also help shape her into the woman she becomes.

Like Vanessa, we have all cried ourselves to sleep at night to be able to wear a smile the next morning for the world. We've all gotten fed up and gone a little "Waiting to

Exhale" crazy on our significant others. We've all been there and we're not alone.

Not only can love hurt, but bras can hurt. High heels can hurt. Our menstrual cycle can hurt. Miscarriages hurt. Child birth hurts. Infertility hurts. Single parenting hurts. Double standards hurt. Sexual harassment hurts. Expectations can hurt. Menopause hurts.

To every woman in the world, let's work to help each other hurt a little less. Let's strive to embrace, uplift, and love each other, because only we know what it's like to walk in our shoes.

Naked Soul

Starring

Karina McNeill as Vanessa **@K.arina_m**

Irishtine Montgomery as Zoe **@Irishbaby___**

Robert Patterson as Chase **@My_Spirit_king_**

Darwin Lewis as Lance **@Theory_of_evolution**

Damon Cheesboro as Abraham **@_Boro**

Shakqueena Bratcher as Ms. Williams **@Nurse_pyt**

Please be sure to check out *Naked Soul's* official trailer.

YouTube: Naked Soul Trailer

https://youtu.be/ccVQBJ9VXfA

Naked Soul: The Zoelyn Story

Chapter 1: Zoe

As summer fades away and a new season approaches, the hours of daylight sadly shorten. The grey skies rush in too early, making it dark and dreary. It has become more and more difficult to navigate through this danger zone alone. The only beauty around me is the vibrant colors of the autumn leaves as they fall and crackle underneath my feet. I hope to one day be whisked out of this poverty, just as the autumn leaves are whisked away by the wind.

I pray for a better life, but God doesn't hear me. I am desperate to escape this place. This home is not a home. Friends aren't invited in because at any time a stray bullet might pierce through the window. I live in the ghetto. I live in the projects of East New York, where drugs and violence are prominent. Where you have to watch your back before someone stabs you in it—and then don't think they're finished. They'll pull that same knife out of you and slit your throat with it, making sure you took your last breath.

I glance around nervously at the men, all dressed in oversized clothes. Some of them I know and some I've never seen before. I, too, am dressed in oversized clothes. For them it's the trend but for me it's for protection. My father's protection. I can't embrace the early stages of womanhood as I near them because the hood is undressing me with its eyes. To avoid being harassed, or even raped, I have to make myself unattractive.

These men stand strong like soldiers, but they don't have the hearts of soldiers -- theirs are the hearts of criminals. They guard their surroundings with their hands at their waists.

Uncle Camo holds an Uzi submachine gun while others hold five vicious pit bulls on leashes. The dogs' fearful gazes and aggressive stances tell me they're about to attack to defend their territory. They bark fiercely, all except for one. The king of the pack. He stands erect, tail up straight, drawing his mouth back in an aggressive snarl. As he exposes his teeth, the blue bandanna tied around his neck somehow comes loose and falls to the ground.

All of a sudden, something doesn't feel right. I tell myself to run but my legs don't move fast enough. From my right, I recognize my father's voice yelling, "Zoelyn run, get down! Get down now!"

Do I run or do I get down? I freeze. My heart is racing fast and I feel it in my neck and chest. Pulsing everywhere.

My ears ring when the first bullet sounds, like an M-80 firecracker being set off, but it's nowhere near the Fourth of July. My stomach is in knots. Sweat races down my face. I can't believe I am just standing here.

If this was a movie, I'd be the girl watching from the couch in living room yelling "Run, you dumb bitch! Run!" Instead it's my father yelling from the other side of the fence.

The chaos surrounding me quickly fades into the background as I look up, but I'm quickly blinded by a glare. A shadow runs towards me at full speed. If the hood weren't only good for breeding criminals my father would be an Olympic athlete or maybe a football player. Yeah, a football player. He sure was built like one.

He runs faster than the speeding bullet that would have probably struck me had he not tackled me to the ground. My head hits the concrete as I fall. We are not players on a football field. There is no gear to protect us from any injuries. This is real life shit.

Everything seems to move in slow motion. I think I'm shot. I think I'm dead already, and don't plan on fighting for my life. But my father is fighting. He uses his body to shelter me from the bullets. For the first time ever, I feel the fear in his heart as he rests his body on top of mine.

When the last shots echo into silence, I feel as though I've been shaken from a panic attack. I am covered in blood. The aggressive pit bull king lies next to me, looking hopeless. His bark has now turned into a cry for help. He took a bullet for me.

While we lie there, Daddy whispers to me, "When I tell you to run, you keep running until you get upstairs and you do not look back. No matter what happens. Understand?"

I am only ten years old. I don't understand. How can I understand? "Come with me, Daddy. Run with me. Don't leave me."

"I have to handle something, but I'm going to be right behind you, Zoe. Just listen to me." He lifts his head to check our surroundings, and when they're clear, he yells, "Run now!"

I book it, running for the door to our building, which is open because the slam lock is broken, as usual. The perks of living in the projects, I guess.

Even though he told me to keep running, I stop for a second and peek through the door to see if he's okay. He's standing there with Uncle Camo, Daddy's best friend. It looks like they're arguing over something but I can't say for sure. The sound of police sirens assures me that the turf war is over and that Daddy will be upstairs soon, so I get into the elevator and hold my breath. Daddy and I always played "Who Can Hold Your Breath The Longest" in the elevator because it always smelled like urine.

As the elevator doors close, I make eye contact with my dad and smile at him, not knowing it will be for the last time. One last shot rings out as I witness Uncle Camo shoot my father, taking away the only person I have, the only man I would ever love.

The elevator doors close too fast for me to race out, but

at the first stop, I get off and rush to the stairway, trying to get to him as quickly as possible. As I'm running down, I pass Uncle Camo who's running up, trying to escape to a safe zone. He's covered in my father's blood.

At this point I'm hysterically crying. I feel my dad's presence as I hear his voice in my head. "My daughter, you are smart. Play it cool or he will kill you too."

I feel unnerved. The man who had practically helped raise me was now my enemy. "Oh my God, Uncle Camo. Are you okay?" It's the first time I've ever seen saw Camo cry, and his tears are fake and insincere. "Where's my dad?"

He kneels down to my level so he can wrap his arms around me. "I'm so sorry, Zoe. Your dad didn't make it. I tried. I tried everything."

I see right through his crocodile tears, but as much as I want to confront him about it, I know I can't. Instead, I have to comfort the man who killed my father.

By the time I make it downstairs, yellow tape is wrapped around the building, making it a crime scene. Helicopters hover overhead while the media swarms, filming and interviewing neighbors. That's when I see my father, whose face was being covered with a white sheet.

I try to run to him, but a detective uses all her strength to hold me back from disrupting her crime scene. "Daddy, please!" I cry out in agony. "Wake up! Wake up! You said you would never leave me."

Daddy's entire crew is dead on the ground except for Uncle Camo, who is peeking out of the window. He is the only one alive.

It was the day that changed my life forever.